THE COMING OF FABRIZZE

THE COMING OF

FABRIZZE

BY RAYMOND DECAPITE

FOREWORD BY TONY ARDIZZONE

Black Squirrel Books

Kent, Ohio

Black Squirrel Books
The Black Squirrel Books imprint includes new nonfiction
for the general reader as well as reprints of valuable studies of Ohio
and its people, including historical writings, literary studies,
biographies, and literature.

Library of Congress Catalog Card Number 2009045843
ISBN 978-1-60635-028-7
Manufactured in the United States of America

First published by David McKay Company, Inc., 1960.

Library of Congress Cataloging-in-Publication Data
DeCapite, Raymond.
The coming of Fabrizze / by Raymond DeCapite ;
foreword by Tony Ardizzone.
p. cm.
Originally published: New York : D. McKay Co., 1960.
ISBN 978-1-60635-028-7 (pbk. : alk. paper)∞
1. Immigrants—Fiction.
2. Italian Americans—Fiction.
3. Railroad construction workers—Fiction.
4. Working class—Fiction.
5. Cleveland (Ohio)–Fiction.
I. Title.
PS3554.E17748C66 2010
813'.54—dc22
2009045843

British Library Cataloging-in-Publication data are available.
14 13 12 11 10   5 4 3 2 1

"I was watching for you."

FOREWORD

IF you agree that one of the truest delights of reading fiction involves the encounter of an engaging narrative voice—a style that rings in your head with an arresting melody and compels you to continue to turn a book's pages when the matters of life call you away—then you'll absolutely love Raymond DeCapite's novel *The Coming of Fabrizze*. Even after half a century—*The Coming of Fabrizze* was first published in 1960—this absolute gem of a novel remains fresh. The story of a community of Italian immigrants who settle on the South Side of Cleveland during the 1920s and put their hands to work laying track for the mighty railroad heading west, DeCapite's debut novel is a book for the ear, a joyous celebration of voices, a sweet American hymn. Rendered largely through crisp declarative sentences and the rhythmic dialogue of its many colorful characters, *The Coming of Fabrizze* is an ethnic classic, the story of Italian immigrants who came to these shores and built America.

The novel focuses on a single young man, who eventually becomes a community organizer and leader, Fabrizze. Named Cennino by his father, the young man yearns to go west and tails the older Augustine, a bird of passage who returns to his village in the mountains of Abruzzi (now Abruzzo) after eight years of hard labor in America. Here, the mythic father accepts the young man and anoints him with a new and powerful name.

It was true. Now and then Augustine heard that soft dancing footfall. He would turn in the cobbled street. The young man had withdrawn into a doorway. Suddenly he stepped forth. His golden hair held the sun and his blue eyes were big with wonder.

"Why is it you follow me?" said Augustine, startled by the shining look of him.

"I like to be with you."

"You're mixing it up. I'm not your father."

"He went away. He wrote a letter about a wild horse."

"I heard about that horse," said Augustine.

"He said he woke one morning and the horse was pounding outside the door. He jumped on and rode away."

viii

"He left you here to starve," said Augustine.

"We were starving when he was here."

"At least you have the truth of it," said Augustine. "And I don't like this name he gave you. It's for a boy and not a man. It's better if you answer only to Fabrizze. Say it for me."

"Fabrizze."

"It's Fa-breets-eh!" said Augustine. "The stroke of an axe."

"Fabrizze!"

"Fabrizze!"

"Fabrizze!"

Though some may believe that most or all Italian immigrants left their native land with the hope of settling in the New World, only a fraction actually did; indeed, from 1907 to 1911 seventy-three out of every one hundred Italians who arrived in the United States returned to Italy. Caught between two worlds, these became known as "birds of passage." Even though three-quarters of all Italian immigrants were farmers or worked for a share of the crops grown on another's land, most immigrants who came to America didn't want to farm in the New World since farming implied a firm commitment to place that the immigrants were not willing to make. Instead they headed to the cities, where jobs were plentiful. They left their wives and families behind, sending money home whenever they could.

Augustine takes Fabrizze with him to the New World and helps him get a job on the railroad. Though later on Augustine returns to his beloved Italy (in response to a friend pointing out that Augustine comes and goes, comes and goes, and asking him where it will all end, Augustine sadly gazes down at the weight of his work shoes and responds, "The end of it? In the end I'll have no home at all."), Fabrizze burns with energy and ambition and rushes headlong into America's bright promise.

Home was the red rooming house on Harrison Street. Fabrizze and Augustine shared room and bed on the seventh floor. They shared everything else with some fifty other immigrants packed together for warmth in the New World

"What smells and dialects!" said Augustine.

No doors were closed in the day. People wandered through the halls. Long into the summer night there was talk running from window to open window. Augustine had the curious feeling that if something happened to one of them it would happen to all of them. He soon decided it was already happening.

"They dream and dream," he told Fabrizze. "I had supper with Penza on the second floor. The man who works with us. I was telling him how bad it is here in America. He put his finger on his lips. He doesn't want to hear about it. He has two shirts. He wears one and washes the other. He has a hole in his shoe. But in a few years he'll send for a wife. 'Look at this place,' I said. He put the finger on his lips. He has a window in the room. He looks out and it's good. There's a boy next door who plays the harmonica. The music is good. 'Wake up,' I said. He put the finger on his lips."

x

"I understand it," said Fabrizze. "Something is in the air. It makes you want to run. It's exciting."

"It's garlic and codfish," said Augustine.

The immigrants soon follow the charismatic Fabrizze as he rises through the ranks. A supervisor puts him in charge of the men on his crew for a day or two, and under Fabrizze's direction the men work so hard and well that soon Fabrizze is put in charge of maintenance and track repair. He rewards Augustine by giving him a pleasant job as day watchman, then works so diligently he is promoted again. Everyone decides that Fabrizze is in need of a wife, and what ensues is a delightful episode about introductions and courtships, culminating with Fabrizze's marriage to a woman named Grace. Fabrizze is put in charge of hiring, and soon a long line of Italian immigrants appears outside Fabrizze's house. Characteristically, he invites each man inside for a glass of wine, hiring as many as the railroad can bear.

Fabrizze also sends his money back to Abruzzi to enable others to come to Cleveland, where, he assures them, a job on the railroad will be waiting for them. He helps others in the community find wives and husbands. Fabrizze and Grace's grandfather, Mendone, go down into Fabrizze's basement and begin making wine.

Jugs were hidden everywhere. Fabrizze and Mendone filled strange black bottles with a blend so imaginative that neither of them could remember the ingredients. They boiled the corks and drove them in and buried the black bottles under the basement floor.

They drank a toast from the first barrel. Something was lacking in there. They went on tasting and mixing. Deep into the night Grace heard the bubbling and pouring and whispering.

"Must you lose sleep with this wine?" she said.

"Wine, wine," said Mendone, frying sausages in it.

"Wine warms you in the winter," said Fabrizze. "Wine cools you in the summer."

"Wine helps the digestion," said Mendone. "Wine enriches the blood. Wine is good for the skin."

"Wine puts a certain light in the eyes," said Fabrizze.

"Is it good for the lungs?" said Grace. "The baby cries out when I take him in the fresh air."

"Wine keeps the teeth clean," said Mendone.

"And it loosens the tongue," said Grace.

"But then it relieves the heart," said Fabrizze.

"And fills our pockets," said Mendone.

Fabrizze and Mendone then open a store filled with sausages and cheeses, olives and horse beans, wild onions and sleeping snails. In the store window they hang a picture of Augustine, taken when he was young. As even more profits mount more money is sent back to Italy, which in turn allows more immigrants to make the passage to the New World. In this way *The Coming of Fabrizze* is both a social history as well as a testament to the ethnic muscle and sweat that not only built but also shaped the character and soul of America.

Fabrizze's financial interests turn, inevitably, to the stock market. Given the novel's time period—the 1920s—you can well imagine what happens next as the charismatic leader of this thriving Italian community agrees to collect funds from everyone and then invests everything in the stock market, making everyone, at least on paper, rich. There are plans to use the money to build houses for more immigrants and thereby expand the community. In the end, after the Wall Street crash of 1929, rather than taking everyone down with him, Fabrizze sacrifices everything he and Grace own so that others in the community might not suffer as badly. Like the hardworking father who is killed in a construction site accident on Good Friday in Pietro di Donato's brilliant *Christ in Concrete,* Fabrizze sacrifices himself so that others— his family—might benefit. He then disappears, and those left behind begin to tell stories about him and say that the day he will return will be "like a feast day." They say that when Fabrizze comes back he'll bring the band from the church, and in celebration they'll string lights up and down the street and make a festa.

Born in Cleveland in 1924, DeCapite served in the United States Coast Guard between 1942–1945 and later earned a bachelor's degree and a master of arts degree from Case Western Reserve University. *The Coming of Fabrizze* was praised by *The New York Times* as "a modern folk tale filled with love, laughter and the joy of life. . . . Reading these merry pages is something like eating a dinner of the very best spaghetti and meat sauce with plenty of Chianti and a string orchestra nearby playing 'Santa Lucia.'" The *New York Herald Tribune* wrote of the novel, "The wine flows incessantly. The music never stops. You can all but smell the sausage and onion frying right out there on the printed page." *Kirkus Reviews* reported, "What distinguishes this almost mythic tale of an immigrant—who succeeds by virtue of hard work and honesty—from other diaspora narratives is not only its good-natured tone, but its poetic language," and goes on to praise the novel's "amazing ear for the lyrical patterns of everyday speech." The novelist John Fante called DeCapite "a writer of exquisite talents." In 1962 *The Coming of Fabrizze* was awarded the prestigious Cleveland Arts Prize for Literature. DeCapite has also been the recipient of the Ohioana Award and the Cleveland Critics' Circle Award, and his work has inspired his son Michael not only to become a writer but also to found his own publishing company, Sparkle Street of San Francisco.

The Coming of Fabrizze puts Raymond DeCapite squarely in the company of the very best Italian American writers: Pietro di Donato, John Fante, Jerre Mangione, and Helen Barolini. Indeed, as Fabrizze himself might suggest, we might drop the qualifying adjective and list DeCapite as among the best American writers of his time.

Delight in the story. Allow yourself to be charmed by the characters. Read favorite passages aloud to family and friends. *The Coming of Fabrizze* is a classic.

Tony Ardizzone

THE COMING OF FABRIZZE

I

SWEET was the welcome for Augustine. Surely it carried an expression of love and longing for America. All his friends followed his mother and nephew down the mountain to meet him in the sunlight. His mother wept. The watchful men saved their smiles until he came to them. Women with eyes like jewels were moving in to squeeze his hand. Several of them held babies up to be admired and then they slipped away behind their men. An old woman called down a greeting from the edge of the village square. Suddenly everyone was shouting his name. Augustine would remember the sound of it ringing through the mountains of Italy.

"Eight years, eight years," he used to say. "I worked like a horse for eight long years. I swore to come home and tell the truth about America. And then what happened? One kiss from the village and I surrendered on the spot."

So it was that peace came to him in the year after the First War ended. And yet he gave no peace to the village of Rivisondoli. It seemed that the one kiss turned him into a lover of America. By the time that he left home again he had enriched the local myth in a way that stamped him a man of high imaginative power. Friends would send for him to hear his glowing account of life in the New World. It was like a song. His voice grew ever stronger with it. His brown eyes would close and his nostrils dilate at the sudden overwhelming fragrance of his "lost bride, America." It was said that Augustine had three varying accounts of his rise to power in America. There were two more accounts, quite as thrilling, of his rise to power over two charming widows right in Rivisondoli.

No one remarked on the fact that his hands were swollen with work. At home Augustine would put his hands on the kitchen table and gaze in silence at his mother.

"Please, Augustine, please," said Rosa. "Must we look at your hands again tonight? Put them away. I understand that you worked. A man lives and he works."

The truth is, Augustine had lived in America as though in a cocoon. He worked for the railroad and hoarded his money. Room and laundry cost him eight dollars a month. He spent about thirty cents a week for food and so his diet never changed. He paid five cents for a bag of white beans, or lentils, and then bought three pounds of the cut odds and ends of spaghetti for nine cents. The grocery clerk was fascinated by him.

"What is it this week?" the clerk would say, in Italian. "Is it the beans again?"

"The lentils," said Augustine. "Are you really an Italian? It's a long way from home, eh?"

The clerk was filling the bag.

"Wait, wait," said Augustine. "I was thinking here. Let it be the beans then. Do you mind?"

The clerk emptied the bag and started with beans.

"Wait, wait," said Augustine. He mopped his brow as though on the verge of panic. "Be kind enough to change to the lentils. How sorry I am. Really, I don't know what's happening to me. It's the living alone that does it. You said beans, my boy, and I found myself saying beans just to show my affection for you. But I settled on the lentils before I came in. I must make my own decision."

Sympathizing, the clerk threw in an extra handful.

Augustine cooked the lentils and spaghetti in a fine tomato sauce seasoned with garlic and parsley and basil leaf. Five days he ate from the same pot, and with the same crazed appetite. When he reached bottom a wild exultant cry would escape him and bring the landlady flying up the stairs to his room.

"How you frightened me!" said Josephine. "What does it mean, Augustine, what does it mean?"

"It's of no importance," said Augustine. "A thing that comes out now and then. Don't upset yourself, my dear."

"Give me warning," said Josephine, piteously. "Let me

5

prepare myself a little. It freezes me to the bone. And my sister almost choked on a piece of beef."

"A piece of beef," said Augustine.

"What can I tell you?" said Josephine. "It's like a terrible thing is loose to devour us all. Will it happen again?"

"Toward the end of the week," said Augustine.

Josephine thought about it.

"Perhaps you should find a wife," she said. "How about the butcher's daughter? She has uncommon strength and beauty. You can take hold of such a girl. Let me arrange it. She'll be tickled to have you."

"Very nice, very nice," said Augustine. "But I can't afford a wife. You forget the people back home."

"But they expect too much of you," said Josephine. "Are you to sacrifice your life for them?"

"I am in chains," said Augustine, huskily. And here he put his hand to his throat and began to choke himself.

"Poor soul," said Josephine.

Augustine had let it be known everywhere that he was the sole support of his mother and his nephew. Thus he was overwhelmed with food and drink when he made his round of visits in the neighborhood. At least once a week he turned up for supper at the house of his railroad foreman Rossi.

"Take a glass of wine with me," Rossi would say. "We were just going to have supper. A glass of wine."

"You don't mean it?" said Augustine, with hapless brown eyes on the floor. He was holding a hat which looked as if it had been used to beat out a fire.

6

"Of course I mean it," said Rossi, flushed with wine. "And I want you to take supper with us."

"It's a trick," said Augustine, in his innocent way.

"What a fellow he is," said Rossi, throwing up his hands. "I tell you, Augustine, you don't leave this house till you take food to warm you. Do you hear me? I say I won't let you out the door. Nancy, snap the lock on the door."

"I believe you mean what you say," said Augustine, musing and stroking his chin. "You speak from the heart. And yet I was on my way home this very minute to bake a loaf of bread."

"He makes his own bread," said Rossi. "Nancy, Nancy. Come and listen to this."

"Perhaps I'll stay the next time," said Augustine.

"I'm giving an order," said Rossi. "Why, it's a curse to eat alone. Stay, stay. Talk a little. Tell me about things in the old country. Your people are from the Abruzzi, eh? How well I know it. The mountains, Augustine, the mountains! First thing in the morning your eyes lift up and your heart pounds!"

"I am in chains," said Augustine.

"But I know about you," said Rossi. "I know how you do without things for your family. Your landlady told me. You give your heart away and all the while you count your beans. I was thinking about you. The way you live gets me excited. It's going through me like a music. You're living like a saint!"

"Like a spider," said Augustine.

Suddenly his nostrils dilated.

7

"Is it hot sausage we're having?" he said, unable to control himself any longer.

"If I could only paint your picture, Augustine, if I could only catch the look of such a man! Nancy, do you see it there? Look, look! It's around the eyes! My name would live forever!"

Sausage was hissing in the oven.

"Good, good," Augustine was saying, softly.

"Forever and ever!" said Rossi. "Such devotion and sacrifice! It's a look of the spirit!"

Sausage was sizzling and popping.

"Wonderful," said Augustine.

"In a class by yourself," said Rossi. "Think how many people depend on you! A lion would break his teeth on such a man!"

"A bit of meat," said Augustine.

"We'll talk later over the wine," said Rossi.

"If you wish."

"You are mine, Augustine!" said Rossi. "My prisoner! I'll have the secret of your strength before the night is done! Nancy, Nancy: snap the lock on the door!"

"Augustine snapped it," said Nancy.

"The mountains, the mountains," said Rossi.

DURING those bleak years Augustine moved between the railroad yard and his lonely room as though dragging a cart. It seemed that his life was reduced to shoveling and sleeping. He was fixed so fast that he carved his initials in a shovel and would sulk all day if someone took it by mistake.

"A man made sick," he said.

He failed to recover until his return to Rivisondoli. Friends were waiting to celebrate his arrival. They marched him up the mountain and danced him through the streets into his home. On the way up Augustine was made well, and made so dangerously well it was a kind of affliction. Certain it is that he was instantly alert to the wonder surrounding his adventures in the New World.

"I discovered America when I came home," he said.

Serenity came to his spirit. He took to strolling round the town and lounging in the cool clean square. Villagers came out of their way to listen to him. Children followed him.

"Tell us something," they would say.

Augustine sipped red wine under the chestnut trees and for a time he was speaking almost in parables. It took him half the morning to walk one block to the square. Sporting a cane he tapped his idling way through the narrow cobbled streets. Windows were opened. Women leaned on sills and called down to him with restlessness and longing in their voices.

"Augustine, Augustine," said Filomena. "Is it true what you say about this America? You're making it up, eh? Come now, tell the truth for once."

"Say my name," said Augustine, leaning on his cane. "Say it again, Filomena."

"Augustine?"

"You make a question and my answer is yes."

"O, Augustine."

"A revelation," said Augustine. "Yes, my dear, most of it is true about America. Except some things. But most of it is true."

"Except some things," said Filomena. "Come and have a bit of coffee then. Arturo is in the fields."

"And he is smiling," said Augustine, going in. "A rare one, Arturo. A provider. Work is the bread of the soul."

"I'll tell Arturo when he comes," said Filomena. "But how is it you brought no woman from America? Are they good to look at?"

"There are no women like the women of Abruzzi. You are born on the heights and it's where you belong. Listen then. Do you know that everyone used to ask why Arturo had the little smile at the corner of the mouth?"

"He has that smile," said Filomena.

"He was smiling at the funerals, too," said Augustine. "And then he grew the moustache to hide it. But we knew he was still smiling. Now I know why he smiles and smiles. I guessed it when you looked at me with those blue eyes. Tell me what you see in mine. Look closer."

Augustine sipped the hot black winy coffee. Presently he was reaching over to pinch her cheek and chin and thigh.

"You mustn't, Augustine, you mustn't."

"I was a fool," said Augustine. "I thought the mountains shut the world out. Now I see they may shut a world in."

"Augustine!"

"A little fun," said Augustine.

10

"It isn't right."

"A little play," said Augustine.

"But we're getting beyond that age."

"Where do you get this information?" said Augustine. "Come down the mountain later. I'll be hiding in the forest. Hunt me down, my dear. . . . Tell Arturo I was asking after him."

Augustine paid several more calls and then he drifted into the quiet little square. He sat in the brilliant sun and watched Umberto putting up, brick by brick, the first hotel in the village.

"Come and take a glass of wine," said Augustine.

"No time, my friend. Each brick is a brick less."

"Or more," said Augustine. "Do you never rest?"

"Never."

"Listen a moment. What if someone came to tell you that you were going on a journey? A far long journey, you understand, from which you'd never return."

"I'd make ready."

"Do it then," said Augustine.

"I'm going nowhere."

"And I say you should make ready."

Appetite fully awake in the nipping mountain air, Augustine strolled homeward for lunch and an afternoon of meditation. Here and there the faces of children were vivid and startling as flowers. Augustine stopped to look into the eyes of a radiant little girl. With his cane he drew a circle round her beauty. He was moving on when he heard Don Antonio calling to him from the church.

"A word with you," said Don Antonio, coming down.

"I've been watching you, my friend. I'm beginning to see the color in your face again. You were so thin and pale when you returned."

"It was a ghost you saw," said Augustine.

"It's good to have you home," said Don Antonio. "You'll share a fine harvest with us. It will be better than last year. And next year, we pray, will be even better."

"Don Antonio, this is my home," said Augustine. "I left here and the people were eating bread and pasta. They're still eating bread and pasta. You talk of progress, Don Antonio?"

"It's you who talk of progress," said Don Antonio. "I would say there is no progress but in the realm of the spirit."

"And so there is no progress?"

"You're teasing," said Don Antonio.

"A man's diet affects his spirit," said Augustine. "Beans and pasta did a serious thing to me, I'm sure of it."

"Come, come," said Don Antonio.

"I find it impossible to soar, as I used to."

"I'll tell you a secret," said Don Antonio. "Nothing is sweeter than sacrifice."

"The secret is safe with me," said Augustine.

"I see you must have laughter," said Don Antonio. "Will you be going back to America then?"

"Once more perhaps," said Augustine. "I miss my home when I'm there and now I miss this America. I may take my nephew and then I'll return for good."

"Your nephew, your nephew," said Don Antonio, clasping his hands in delight. "Who can resist him?"

"A fine young man," said Augustine.

"He used to sing in church when he was a boy. One day he was singing higher and higher. 'There it is,' I was saying. And then he went higher. The others stopped singing. I was looking the other way. I pretended not to listen."

"He's like a light in the house."

"It will be a great loss for your mother. How is she then?"

"She was praying for me to come home," said Augustine. "And now she's praying for me to take Cennino away."

Augustine was right. One hope Rosa had and it was to get her grandson started in a new life in America. Day and night she argued with Augustine. Thwarted, she put her hands to her temples as though something had caved in on her.

"Everyone talks of going," she said, spitefully.

"But it's not what you think," said Augustine.

"Nor is it what you say," said Rosa. "You sing in the square and with me you talk out of the corner of the mouth. Is it true that hundreds are going from Naples each month? Did you see them in America? How do they fare?"

"Dropping to the left and right as though shot down. There was one who became a sailor. He was going back and forth and in the end he chose the sea. The world outside," said Augustine, pointing to the west.

"Listen then," said Rosa. "Let me tell you about this Cennino. You left a boy here and found a man past twenty. I'll tell you about that boy before you lose him. He did everything for me. He plowed and planted and brought in the grain. He took care of the cow and the pigs. He

13

helped to put up ham and cheese and lard against the winter. And then one year I was sick. Three months in bed with a stiff back. I couldn't move. I couldn't even sit down. He watched me like a baby. In the afternoon he lifted me out of bed and held me in the sun a little. He was up before the light to make bread. And in the night he would read the books that Don Antonio brought from Rome."

"And so you'll send him away," said Augustine.

"All he talks about is this America," said Rosa. "He's ashamed to trouble you with his questions. But he follows you in the day."

It was true. Now and then Augustine heard that soft dancing footfall. He would turn in the cobbled street. The young man had withdrawn into a doorway. Suddenly he stepped forth. His golden hair held the sun and his blue eyes were big with wonder.

"Why is it you follow me?" said Augustine, startled by the shining look of him.

"I like to be with you."

"You're mixing it up. I'm not your father."

"He went away. He wrote a letter about a wild horse."

"I heard about that horse," said Augustine.

"He said he woke one morning and the horse was pounding outside the door. He jumped on and rode away."

"He left you here to starve," said Augustine.

"We were starving when he was here."

"At least you have the truth of it," said Augustine. "And I don't like this name he gave you. It's for a boy and not a man. It's better if you answer only to Fabrizze. Say it for me."

14

"Fabrizze."

"It's Fa-*breets*-eh!" said Augustine. "The stroke of an axe."

"Fabrizze!"

"Fabrizze!"

"Fabrizze!"

A window was opened.

"What's happening?" said Filomena.

"Where, my dear?" said Augustine.

"I keep hearing the name Fabrizze," said Filomena.

"Your condition is interesting," said Augustine. "Put the coffee on and I'll be up in a moment. . . . Go home, Fabrizze. At supper you'll sing for me."

Fabrizze hurried home to help Rosa prepare the supper. They rolled veal in flour and egg and then fried it in olive oil. They toasted mellow bulbs of mozzarella cheese. Rosa cut three great slices of dark sweet bread. There was red wine and strong coffee and little yellow apples.

"He's coming, Nino, he's coming," said Rosa. "Spare him nothing when you sing. Fall to the floor at the end of it. Put your hands on his knees. Pay attention!"

Augustine came in and sat down.

"Sing for your uncle," said Rosa. "His food will taste so much the better. Sing 'Mama.' . . . No mercy, do you hear?"

Fabrizze planted himself six feet away from Augustine. He took aim. Suddenly his voice filled the house. He cried out for his lost mother. His eyes were shut and his face was white with passion. The last wild gesture almost brought Augustine headlong into his arms.

Augustine had dropped his fork. Violent shivers were racing up and down his spine.

"He has no one, poor child, no one at all," said Rosa, clasping her hands. "What's to be done, what's to be done?"

"Give me a kiss," said Augustine. "Your poor mother is dead, my boy, and the song runs me through like a sword."

"What's to be done?" said Rosa, wailing.

Just before he woke each morning Augustine would hear Fabrizze singing in the old stone house. A remembered song seemed to send a silver light into his sleep. Augustine would lie in bed for a long while. From the stable below his room rose the strong homely smell of livestock. A horse went its lazy clip-clop over the cobbles. Men saluted each other in bursts of recognition. Voices were packed with surprise and delight.

"Folino."

"Gullo."

"Rumbone."

They waited to give and take a bit of warmth in the clear tremendous morning. Their eyes were sharp and steady and yet their sudden smiles would melt the heart.

"A bright day," someone would say.

"A light to keep us honest."

The men were going to the fields. Some were dozing as they rode patient little donkeys through the cool streets and down the path. Here and there old women in black were saying the rosary on steps of sunlit stone. Presently the men were free of the village. Everywhere the mountains told a mighty story.

16

"Fabrizze," said Augustine.

Fabrizze brought a cup of black coffee. He sat away from the bed so as not to intrude on his uncle first thing in the morning. Augustine beckoned him closer to feel the warmth and love in those deep soft eyes.

"Listen to me," said Augustine. "It's not true what you hear. You have wrong ideas. . . . Look outside. Do you see how it seems with the sun? The sun must climb the mountains to bring light into this village. Always the same hard climb to win the day. It was the same for me in America."

"But we'll climb together. How I look forward to it!"

"You must forget what I've been telling the people here. It's true enough that America is a good place. For the young it's even better. But it means work. It means work."

"I'm not afraid," said Fabrizze. "I take hold of things with both hands. I push or pull and it's all the same to me. I'm never tired. I love to work."

"You've been at the wine, eh?" said Augustine.

"I'll work for us both."

"All right then," said Augustine. "We'll go and be together for a time. But I'm coming back. I'm getting older and I want a family of my own."

"When will we leave?"

"In the spring of the year."

"The spring, the spring!"

"We'll go to a place called Cleveland. There'll be work on the railroad. Perhaps you can go to school at night. Now you must get some books from Don Antonio. Do things right. Learn the language and the ways of this America. Do it with your heart."

"Which way is it? Which way will we go?"

"After the sun," said Augustine, carried away.

Fabrizze gave a cry and hurried to the kitchen. Rosa took her milky hands from a pail. She was making mozzarella cheese. She stopped to prepare the breakfast. She set forth a dish of sweet white butter in coils. She poured coffee and cream into three cups. As always there was the great loaf of bread with the sign of the cross in it.

"Sing for your uncle," she was saying.

"Stop with this singing," said Augustine, coming in. "It's all settled. I'll take him to America."

"What is it?" said Rosa.

"I say we're going to America."

"But when?" said Rosa, aghast.

"Why so surprised?" said Augustine. "It's the only thing I've been hearing from you."

Rosa rushed outside with hands against temples.

The village shared in the excitement and preparation. There was endless talk about it. A sudden unrest gripped the young men. It seemed they were imprisoned by the dead black wall of mountain. They threatened to leave as soon as they could save the fare. They begged Augustine to send for them. One night the ancient midwife Caterina packed her things and said she was determined to go unless she received better treatment at home.

Fabrizze had everyone speaking a few words of English.

"Hello, hello," he would say.

"Hello, hello," said the neighbor Ferrari.

"And goodbye, goodbye," said Fabrizze.

"And goodbye, goodbye," said Ferrari.

18

Gifts were brought during the winter. Here was a woolen blanket. Consolo made fine strong shoes for them. Someone left an axe. Ferrari came with a sheath of long white underwear for Fabrizze.

"Made by my Anna," said Ferrari. "It will keep the warmth of you inside. You'll remember old Ferrari, eh?"

"And for me," said Augustine. "Is there nothing for me?"

Ferrari gave him a little whip cut from leather.

"For your imagination," he said.

Augustine was troubled. He spent the winter girding himself to act on his decision to leave. The thought of America tied his stomach in a knot.

"I tell you it binds me," he said.

He proclaimed himself sacrificed in advance.

"I feel like an old man," he said. "All my bones ache."

"At the age of forty?" said Rosa.

"This voyage will finish me," he said. "You don't know what it is. They'll put us below the water. Like animals in the dark. What smells and dialects! The women are everywhere putting things in place. And the sea begins to laugh. And the women get sick with it. And then the children get sick. And then the men. I tell you I'm finished."

"Send for Don Antonio," said Rosa.

AUGUSTINE was more cheerful with the coming of spring. The excitement in Fabrizze gave him strength and courage. It would be good to see America once more.

19

"But when will it be?" said Fabrizze.

"Soon enough."

"But when? Please tell me the day."

"One week from tomorrow," said Augustine. "After the feast of Ascension. We'll feast while we can. Two days later we'll start for Naples. Just in time to catch the ship."

And so they set forth on a morning in May.

All doors in the village were open. They stopped again and again to take wine and coffee. By the time they were under way a crowd was following them down the mountain path.

Cipitti played the accordion.

"Augustine, you'll send for me?" said a man called Rumbone.

"Send for me," said another.

"Have a care! He'll send for your wife!"

"All these broken hearts!"

"The church will be full again!"

"Anything to be the ear of Don Antonio!"

Augustine looked over his shoulder. The women were lovely beyond words. Their faces were strong and rosy and their clear eyes were shining with laughter. Augustine glanced up at the village cradled high in the mountains. He saw the clean soar of the church steeple and he thought of the sunny little square and the intimacy of cobbled streets.

"They're really going, eh?" said a voice, sudden and fatal in the crowd.

Rosa was slowing down. She stopped for a moment to

wipe her face with her apron. Augustine and Fabrizze were moving away.

All at once Rosa realized what was happening.

"Madonna mia," she said.

She sank down by the side of the path.

"I'll never see them again," she said.

Two women stayed to comfort her.

Augustine and Fabrizze went on down the mountain.

"And goodbye, goodbye," said Ferrari.

Suddenly Fabrizze was frozen with the agony of parting.

"Uncle, Uncle!"

"Don't stop," said Augustine, taking his arm. "Don't look back any more."

"O my God!" Rosa was sobbing. "The house will be a grave! O my lovely boys! Augustine! Nino, Nino!"

The names echoed down and round the mountains.

II

WEST and west and west," said Augustine. "We marched from the mountains to the sea. We sailed after the sun. Twelve days, twelve days. Finally we landed and took the train. Six hundred miles to the west again. And then one morning Rossi was there. He put his arms around me. 'He makes his own bread,' he was saying. There were tears in his eyes. He had a surprise for me. My shovel was waiting. I cried like a baby. I was calling Fabrizze to help me. He was bringing water in a bucket to the labor gang. It was over for him, too, with his golden hair."

It was beginning.

Fabrizze moved from water boy to laborer on the Great Northern Shore Railroad. Three nights a week he studied the language with an old railroad worker called Bassetti. They bought the newspaper and went through it page by page. Fabrizze never turned up without a bag of oranges for the old man. Toward the end of the summer Bassetti realized that his pupil had become his teacher. He pointed out that the oranges were losing their sweetness now that he gave nothing in return. He made an end of it and sent Fabrizze home.

Home was the red rooming house on Harrison Street. Fabrizze and Augustine shared room and bed on the seventh floor. They shared everything else with some fifty other immigrants packed together for warmth in this New World.

"What smells and dialects!" said Augustine.

No doors were closed in the day. People wandered through the halls. Long into the summer night there was talk running from window to open window. Augustine had the curious feeling that if something happened to one of them it would happen to all of them. He soon decided it was already happening.

"They dream and dream," he told Fabrizze. "I had supper with Penza on the second floor. The man who works with us. I was telling him how bad it is here in America. He put his finger on his lips. He doesn't want to hear about it. He has two shirts. He wears one and washes the other. He has a hole in his shoe. But in a few years he'll send for a wife. 'Look at this place,' I said. He put the finger on his lips. He has a window in the room. He looks out and it's good. There's a boy next door who plays the harmonica. The music is good. 'Wake up,' I said. He put the finger on his lips."

"I understand it," said Fabrizze. "Something is in the air. It makes you want to run. It's exciting."

"It's garlic and codfish," said Augustine. "Rumbone is making supper downstairs. It happens to be where I'm going. We have this plan for you. I want you to keep your eyes open on the job. Go to Bassetti again. Ask him questions about the work on the railroad. Learn everything you can. Be ready."

Rumbone winced when he saw Augustine.

"Just in time for supper," said Rumbone.

"You don't mean it?" said Augustine. "There isn't enough."

"Say no more," said Rumbone.

"Enough for one, enough for two, eh?" said Augustine.

"Enough for one, enough for one," said Rumbone. "Don't mix it up, Augustine. We know each other from the village."

"You run me through," said Augustine. "Pass the fish then."

"I've been thinking about Fabrizze," said Rumbone. "We must let these people know he's there."

"It isn't right for me to take his part," said Augustine.

"I'll take his part," said Rumbone. "I've been watching this Rossi. The man is nervous. I'll bring him down from behind."

Rumbone had the keen look of a hunter. Carefully he set about to stalk the railroad supervisor. He froze in his tracks whenever Rossi came in sight. He gazed in silence. Pale troubled eyes aimed down that blade of a nose.

"You there," said Rossi. "Stop it, stop it."

Rumbone put up his shovel and came over.

"I didn't mean that," said Rossi. "I want you to stop looking at me. I feel unbuttoned with it."

"What is it?" said Rumbone. "Who's unbuttoned?"

"Never mind," said Rossi, starting away. "Back to work."

"What's happening?" said Rumbone, following him. "They told me to stay here. But where you are taking me?"

"Go back to work!" cried Rossi. "What a fool!"

After several weeks of this Rossi took it into his head that Rumbone might be a source of information about the men. Rumbone sensed that the time was ripe. He winked and called the supervisor aside. He asked mysterious questions.

"You see him there?" said Rumbone. "Tell me his name. The one with a face like a big potato."

"You mean Gritti," said Rossi.

"So it's Gritti," said Rumbone. "So it's Gritti then."

"What about him?" said Rossi. "Tell me what happened. Why do you ask about Gritti?"

"Never mind," said Rumbone. "Let's wait a little."

The supervisor warned Gritti to be careful.

A few days later Rumbone was winking again.

"I have news for you," he said. "The pusher knows less than the men. And he works less."

"What pusher?" said Rossi. "There is no pusher here. Wait, Rumbone, wait. Which one said he was a pusher? Show me."

"I see," said Rumbone. "The smoke is clearing."

"Show me this pusher!" cried Rossi.

"It's for us to settle with him," said Rumbone.

Rossi carried the conversation for weeks. He went out of his way to find Rumbone. He listened and listened and heard nothing. One morning he called Rumbone into the tool shed.

"I want you to tell me something," said Rossi. "Let me warn you that everything depends on it. Yesterday my heart was pounding when I saw you. My blood came to a boil. My stomach was all upset when I left you. Now I want to know why. Do you understand me? Speak now or never!"

"I have one more question," said Rumbone. "Where is it you go in the day? Why are you never here?"

"It's not for you to ask," said Rossi. "I make no account to you, my friend."

"You should stay here more," said Rumbone, significantly. "I speak as a friend. Really now, where do you go?"

"Leave me alone!" said Rossi. "There's too much work these days. I have to be near the steel mill. A coke plant is going up. Switch crossings must be put in. . . . A friend, eh? I'm giving you a last chance. Come closer. Do these men talk about me? Do they mock me?"

"They have a little game," said Rumbone. "They pretend you don't exist. . . . My dear Rossi, it's the mark of a leader that he knows how to pick a leader. Isn't it so? Someone to give orders in his absence. Consider it. You take credit for the dance without piping the tune. These men are making a fool of you. I don't like to see it."

26

"Is this the only gang I have?" said Rossi. "Can I be everywhere at once? The work is out of hand. We're short of men. But who is this leader? Is it you? Are you the piper? Tell me, tell me! Let me laugh out loud in your face! Let me laugh a little!"

"No, my friend, no," said Rumbone, with a sneer. "Your leader has iron in him. He understands the work here. He knows a bit of English and he can talk to important men when it's necessary."

"But who is this man? Must I send a ship for him? Speak up, Rumbone. Where is this giant? I'm sick of looking at you!"

Rumbone made a strange little gesture. He drew his fingers up his neck and out under his chin, as if to say, "Not even another look are you worth."

"You mustn't do that to me," said Rossi. "I'm the supervisor and I don't like the look of it. Come closer. Tell me who it is you're talking about."

"Find out yourself," said Rumbone, making the gesture.

"Don't do that!"

"And once more," said Rumbone.

A week later Rumbone cornered him again. He put his hand on Rossi and waited there in silence. He was listening for the leak in the supervisor that was the source of all the trouble. For a moment Rossi was listening.

"But what day is this?" said Rumbone.

"Thursday, Thursday," said Rossi.

"It's a holy day, eh?"

"What holy day?" said Rossi. "What are you saying? Take your hand off me."

"I noticed the men had extra time for lunch," said Rumbone. "I thought it was a saint's day. Just a moment, Rossi. Let me ask you something. It's between the two of us, eh? What time does the work begin here in the morning? Really now. There was a little quarrel among the men."

"Line them up!" cried Rossi. "This miserable crew! Must I be here every minute? Line up, I say! You there! All of you!"

Rossi was surrounded.

"Do you know who I am?" he said, in crisp Italian. "I want you to pay attention! Do you know who's talking to you?"

"It's Rossi, eh?" said a voice.

"Be quiet," said another. "It's the supervisor."

"No talking out of turn!" said Rossi. "Come closer. Look at my right hand! Look here at my right hand! Do you know what's in it? Think a moment! I want you to think a moment!"

"He speaks a dialect from the north."

"North of Rome, be sure of it."

"No talking!" said Rossi. "Do you know what's in this hand of mine? You don't? Let me tell you what's in it! The fate of every man here! Your whole life is in it! Let me tell you that no man makes a fool of Giuseppe Rossi!"

"Not one word of it do I understand."

"Stand back!" said Rossi. "Why are you closing in like this?"

"How nervous he is."

28

"I told you to line up!" said Rossi. "You call this a line? Never mind, never mind! Get away from me! How you make me sick! All I smell is garlic!"

"There was something nasty, eh?"

"How flushed he is."

"Get away!" said Rossi. "It's over! Back to work with you!"

"Not even one word."

"Stand back there!" cried Rossi. "Stop pushing!"

"Stop that pushing."

"It's the supervisor, eh?"

Rossi had pushed two men away. They were pushed back from the rear. Rossi pushed again. There was a curse. An argument started. Suddenly the mass of men began to sway and close in. Rossi's hand went up. He was sucked out of sight. A moment later the crowd came apart. Rossi was down on one knee. He was livid.

"Rumbone, Rumbone," he was saying.

"I'm here," said Rumbone. "Get up, Rossi."

"Rumbone."

"Stand up, Rossi. It isn't right. It isn't right to be seen like this before the men."

"I'm giving an order," said Rossi. "I want the name of the man who'll take charge of these animals. I'm finished with them. This is an order."

"It sounds like a threat," said Rumbone, starting to make his gesture of contempt.

"If you do that once more, Rumbone, I'll break your face! Back to work with you!"

Rossi turned up early the next morning. Like one enthralled he made his way to Rumbone. Rumbone was leaning on a shovel and stroking his chin.

"Hard to believe," he was saying. "Who'd believe it?"

"What is it?" said Rossi, tightly. "Now what is it?"

"Nothing, Rossi, nothing. Why do you get so excited?"

"What's happening here?" said Rossi, making circles in the air with his cupped hand.

"It was a surprise," said Rumbone. "A little surprise."

"I'll strangle you on the spot!"

"But it was nothing at all. One of the men brought wine and a deck of cards to the job. What do you make of it? Wait, Rossi, wait. The time has come."

"It's your time that's come!"

"Listen, listen," said Rumbone. "One word will solve your problems. I want you to look down the line of men digging there. Watch the first eight of them. They dig in the same rhythm, eh? Why is it? The old man Bassetti sings and sets the pace for them. Watch, Rossi, watch."

"I'm falling asleep with it."

"Speak softly," said Rumbone. "You'll wake them."

"Are you telling me to get rid of Bassetti?"

"Why should you?" said Rumbone. "A man must eat whether he works or not. Isn't it so? Besides, he's retiring soon."

"They'll never let him go," said Rossi.

"Now I want you to look down at the end of that line. On the other side. Do you see the golden head? Watch, watch. Up and down twice while the others are down. There is the man who'll set fire to this row."

30

"You mean Fabrizze."

"He is the piper."

"A baby. They'll swallow him up."

"Is he the best worker? Does he know the job?"

"He seems to know it," said Rossi.

"He's a favorite with the men. Try him. It will be the first clever thing you've done in years."

Rossi made the gesture of contempt.

"Are you telling Rossi a new thing?" he said. "I know about this Fabrizze. I've been watching him. Why do you think I'm here so early? To listen to you? Back to work."

Rossi went over and tapped Fabrizze.

"Come aside here," he said.

"I was waiting," said Fabrizze.

"Really?" said Rossi. "Who are you?"

"I am Fabrizze."

"And so everything is settled? You dig as though a treasure is there. Do you know me?"

"You are the supervisor. Your name is Giuseppe Rossi."

"Are you as strong as you look?"

"Strong as a bull," said Fabrizze. "And more intelligent."

"Did you hear my speech yesterday?"

"It put a chill in my bones," said Fabrizze. "You handle the language like a whip. Near the end your voice would've filled a cathedral. It was when you explained that we were in the palm of your hand."

"I'm outnumbered here," said Rossi, scratching his head. "So you say that you're intelligent? Do you know what a stock rail is? What is the function of a frog? What

31

is the best ballast for the ties? Can you put in a switch crossing? Can you get work from a pack of buffoons?"

"No one wakes me in the morning," said Fabrizze. "Sharp at five all the blood rushes to my head. I'm ready for anything. I can run straight to the top of a mountain."

"I can hardly climb to the bathroom," said Rossi.

"There's a black dog in the neighborhood. He follows me when I leave the house. He knows I'm on the track of a big thing."

"Now I remember you," said Rossi. "The nephew of Augustine. The mountains, my boy. You've come from the mountains."

"I have a cup of earth from a mountain near my home. I breathe deep when I look at it."

"Stop a moment," said Rossi. "Save your strength. Listen to me. I'm putting you in charge of the men for a day or two. Do you think you can build a number ten switch down by the water pump? Can you do it right and good? You are so young, my boy, that I must show evidence of your ability to the superintendent. Come along and I'll explain what I want. Afterwards you can go home and think it through. Tomorrow you stand or fall."

The next morning Rossi came to lend a hand. He stood there stunned. Fabrizze was whirling in the midst of the men.

"The switch rails are measured," he was saying. "I measured them while you slept. You men keep grading. We start the spiking right away. Get the clamps ready. This rail is to be cut."

A rail was set on the angle bar. Cardino cut through it

with a blow torch. Fabrizze helped his men lift the rail high before dropping it to break the end off.

"Everybody run," said Fabrizze, dropping the rail. "Everybody come back. Leave the torch on. Put a hole here. This goes from the switch point to the rail of the frog!"

"To the frog," said Rumbone.

"What dialect is this?" said Gritti.

"Along the stock rail," said Fabrizze. "Watch the guard rail. Ready with the fish plate. In at the joint. Keep tamping."

"The fish plate," said Augustine.

"Start with the spiking," said Fabrizze. "Gritti works without singing. Keep singing. Watch the lip on that rail. Put the rails in tight. They'll shrink in the cold. Up on the angle bar. Cut where the line is. Everybody lift. Everybody run. Leave the torch on. Put a hole here."

Suddenly Fabrizze was dashing down to the dispatcher.

"Open the westbound," he said. "The main line is open."

He hurried back.

"Here he comes," said Cardino, dropping the torch.

The men stopped in their tracks as though beset.

"Why dig so deep?" said Fabrizze, to the shovelers. "What are you burying? Save your strength. Get ready with the spikes. This to be cut. Around the knuckle. Up on the angle bar. Everybody lift. Everybody run. Penza runs without lifting. Leave the torch on. Put a hole here. And here and here!"

Rossi left to make his rounds.

No one was in sight when he returned. The switch

gleamed in the sun. Fabrizze and Augustine came out of the tool shed.

"Where are the men?" said Rossi. "Did you bury them?"

"They worked well and so I sent them home," said Fabrizze.

"We'll see about this," said Rossi.

He crawled over the seventy-seven feet of switch. He studied every inch of it. He stood up and scratched his head. For a moment it seemed he would get down and crawl over it again.

"Nothing is hidden," said Fabrizze, laughing. "It's there in the sun for you."

"But how did you get such work out of them?" said Rossi.

"It was stored up," said Fabrizze. "These men were saving and saving and all restless with it. I helped them to spend a little. I challenged them. I asked if they came six thousand miles to play in the sand with their shovels. 'So it seems,' said Gritti. But then one of the others came forward. How angry he was. 'I for one say no!' he cried. He threw his shovel aside. The rest of the men were excited. 'Follow me,' I said. 'This morning we'll sign our name with a fine switch crossing.' And there it is."

"Wait, wait," said Rossi. "Who was it came forward?"

"A man from Abruzzi," said Augustine.

"He's called Rumbone," said Fabrizze. "Such pride!"

"Come along and take supper with me," said Rossi. "And bring your uncle. I want to keep an eye on him."

"The mountains, the mountains," said Augustine.

"They fell on me," said Rossi.

34

FABRIZZE was put in charge of maintenance and track repair from the Yale Bridge down ten miles to United Steel. Fifteen men followed him. Each day they followed him closer. Augustine became a watchman. Fabrizze arranged the pleasant job when he heard his uncle speak of a return to Italy.

"I don't understand this job," said Augustine. "Who was the watchman before me?"

"The men took turns," said Fabrizze. "Now the job is yours. You'll watch the tool shed. You must be here early in the morning to open the shed and pass out the tools. Here is the key. What a relief to put the burden on you."

"And after I pass out the tools?"

"Be ready for anything," said Fabrizze. "Watch, watch. Today you can watch for rain. See how cloudy it is?"

"And if it rains?"

"Shut the door and stay inside," said Fabrizze. "Come out later and watch for the rainbow. I'm leaving now with the men. We'll be back for lunch. Are you watching?"

"Like a bulldog," said Augustine. "I'm watching for the one who'll come to steal this job."

Rumbone assumed the title of chief assistant to the section foreman. It gave him the right to repeat orders.

"Come with me," Fabrizze would say. "Come with me for something different. A new thing for us. It's like an adventure. We must get to the bottom of the rubbish cars."

"Rubbish cars," said Rumbone. "An adventure."

35

"Stop, Rumbone, stop," said Gritti. "Do you really think it's an adventure in the rubbish cars?"

"I believe what the foreman says," said Rumbone.

"It's different when he says it," said Gritti. "Control yourself. Not everyone should walk the rope."

Fabrizze was irresistible. Several of his men lived in the red rooming house and they would pound his door early in the morning. They came to fetch him for work. Shouts were heard as they swept him like a prize into the railroad yard. His success was startling evidence of the opportunity in America.

"Is it Fabrizze?"

"Come this way, my boy. I have white cake for you."

Penza was following Fabrizze.

"I had a look at the switch," said Penza, in his quiet confiding way. "It's over a month now. It will outlast us all."

"Come along to the shed," said Fabrizze. "We'll leave our lunches there and have a bit of coffee. Let's see if my uncle is on duty. Penza, Penza! What a watchman we have!"

Augustine was standing snug between two vertical beams in the darkest corner of the shed. Fast asleep, he was facing the other way with hands driven into pockets.

"How resourceful," said Fabrizze, softly. "Look at him. Will he oversleep at home in a warm bed? Never, never. He comes at dawn to open the shed for us. Duty, Penza, duty."

"There is something in what you say," said Penza. "Myself, I wouldn't have seen it in just that light. He's sleeping, eh?"

36

"No, my friend, no," said Augustine, working loose from between the beams. "I'm watching every move you make."

"How cunning," said Fabrizze. "We should go on tiptoe here. What a watchman!"

"But does he watch all day?" said Penza. "The men complain that food is missing from their lunches. All the best of it, too. Gritti's cake was taken. A peach was stolen from Cardino. I was missing a green pepper with olive oil inside."

"What kind of thief is this?" said Augustine. "Show your face! Who dares to steal bread from men sweating in the sun?"

"It isn't the bread," said Penza. "It's the cake and other sweet things."

"I'll never rest," said Augustine. "I'll track him to the end of the earth. I'll catch him by the hair and swing him round my head. We need more evidence."

"Today I brought two of the green peppers," said Penza.

"With oil?" said Augustine.

"With oil," said Penza. "I was hoping the thief would leave me one. What do you think?"

"Time will tell," said Augustine.

"On guard," said Fabrizze. "Come along then, Penza. I have news for the men. . . . Listen, everyone, listen. Come closer. I have a surprise for you."

"It's the slag dump," said Gritti.

"No, no," said Fabrizze. "The men at the steel company sent word to Rossi. Switch crossings are needed down by the new coke plant. Do you know they chose us to do the work? One of them heard we'll save time and money. And Rossi is giving us a chance with it."

Rossi came by to supervise. He began to circle the group of men. Closer and closer he came. Suddenly he was making a wider circle. It looked like an escape.

"There's no way in, eh?" said Cardino.

"And no way out," said Gritti.

"Leave the torch on!" said Fabrizze.

"It begins again," said Cardino.

Rossi watched from a distance. He went away for lunch and came back with the superintendent. The next morning they were smoking their pipes and watching. Now and again they nodded to each other.

"I knew his uncle before he came," said Rossi.

"Remarkable," said the superintendent. "I was standing behind him. He turned around. His hair is like flame and still you see the blue of his eyes. And then it's his nose. It was holding me there. I couldn't move."

"I started him as a water boy," said Rossi. "The men would call for water just to look at him. He was drowning them."

Along came the chief engineer McGuire. He asked for a pipeful of tobacco. He was watching Fabrizze as he lit the pipe. Smiling, he turned to the superintendent.

"He's good to watch?" said McGuire.

"Good to watch? I almost took my shirt off and got in with him. I was thinking about him last night. I looked forward to seeing him again. I came straight here."

"You have nothing better to do?" said McGuire.

The superintendent left.

"Wait a moment, Rossi," said McGuire. "You should be ashamed of yourself. Didn't I hear that these men were on the verge of a mutiny? No need to hide it. I know they assaulted you. I have sources of information. And here is a young man getting music out of them. Listen to me. I want him left alone on this job."

McGuire was left alone there smoking his pipe.

THE strong intricate web of rail was finished to perfection in three months. Word of it spread through the neighborhood. Friends came in the evening to study it from high on Yale Bridge. Everyone was talking about Fabrizze. The wives of his men learned that his mother was dead. They sent fruit and cake to him in the lunches of their husbands. They offered to do his laundry and mend his socks. It was a time of great happiness.

One day at noon the men gathered for lunch. They sat in the shade of the sycamore tree behind the tool shed. Fabrizze was the center of attention.

"Here is hot pepper for you," said Bassetti. "It will stir the fire in your blood."

"Taste a bit of cheese," said Cardino. "From the province of Calabria. My poor mother makes it with her own hands. She sends it every year, my boy, and it keeps me under her spell. It's my wife who says it."

"Calabria, Calabria," said Fabrizze. "They say you'll never mistake an apple from there."

"Everything is smaller," said Cardino. "Even the men."

"The apples are small and wrinkled," said Fabrizze. "But they are sweet and strong as wine. It's because the earth is poor and they have to fight for life."

"I could listen to this a little longer," said Cardino.

"There's a girl asking about you," said Penza.

"Who is she?" said Fabrizze.

"Her name is Grace. She lives with her grandfather Mendone in the gray house on Jackson Street. What a lovely girl! Black hair. Her eyes are brown and yet you'll see this light of gold if she's pleased. She looks at you and she's all satisfied."

"The carpenter Mancini is after her," said Gritti. "And he made a proposal."

"A bit of advice," said Rumbone. "Waste no time with women. A woman is like an anchor."

"There it is," said Penza, lighting up. "A pepper gone."

"What kind of man is this?" said Augustine. "Who would dare?"

"Someone at the mercy of his appetite," said Bassetti.

"I don't mind," said Penza. "One day he left me both peppers and I was feeling left out of it. How would you say it?"

"The pepper is a bond between you," said Rumbone.

"We'll set a trap," said Augustine. "He's in our midst, be sure of it. Trust no one. Bring another pepper tomorrow. We'll draw him in deeper and deeper."

"I'll bring two again," said Penza.

"With oil, with oil," said Augustine.

"Her people come from Reggio," said Gritti. "It's a city

just across from Sicily. Do you know I come from Sicily?"

"It's your nose that tells us," said Rumbone.

"My nose?"

"They call it the Sicilian nose," said Rumbone. "I saw it in a book once. It's a nose more for use than beauty."

"Look who's talking," said Gritti.

"Sicily, Sicily," Fabrizze was saying, in a puzzled way.

"The word itself is laughter," said Gritti.

"The joke is on you," said Rumbone.

"I believe I've heard of Sicily," said Fabrizze.

"Of course you've heard of it," said Gritti. "Don't listen to them. Sicily is known the world over. We are off by ourselves and washed clean by the sea on all sides. At one time, they say, the famous men of Greece were there."

"It was a Greek who first landed there," said Rumbone. "He had two flags with him. 'I claim it for Greece,' he said. And then he looked again. 'I claim it for Italy instead,' he said. And then he left. And so did you."

"And we're together here," said Gritti. "Can you tell me what the Abruzzi is famous for?"

"Men like me," said Augustine.

"But why did you leave such a place?"

There was a strange moment of silence. Augustine scooped up a handful of earth and let it run through his fingers. He waited for the talk to begin again. He looked at Gritti.

"Why did you leave then?" said Gritti.

"But I'm going back," said Augustine, softly.

Fabrizze started to smile. Suddenly he turned pale.

"Really, Augustine?" said Gritti. "Do you mean it?"

"I want you to stay," said Fabrizze.

"I'll be leaving soon," said Augustine. He kept his glance fixed on Gritti. "I stayed so long only to see him settled."

"What can I tell you?" said Fabrizze. "I want you to stay with all my heart. I thought you changed your mind."

The men were fidgeting.

"There's nothing to say," said Cardino. "But let me say that my wife prepares a sweet thing for the holidays. I'm bringing it to bait a trap."

"You must persuade him to stay," said Fabrizze. "I'm saving to send for my grandmother. We'll be together again."

Helplessly, Fabrizze looked to his men.

"But what is happening?" said Gritti. "First you were there, Augustine, and then you were here. And then you went back. And now you come and go again. Where is the end of it, Augustine?"

Augustine was gazing at his great brown work shoes. He could feel the weight of them pulling him down.

"The end of it?" he said. "In the end I'll have no home at all."

III

SOON after the departure of Augustine it was clear to everyone that Fabrizze needed a wife. He was pouring himself, and his men, into the maintenance work on the railroad. He would sweep into the yard and gather the men and march them here and there like a little army. They put in new ties and repaired the switches. They cleaned out the old ballast on their ten miles of roadbed. They were still marching in the winter and yet it was only to tighten bolts and work up an appetite for lunch. Fabrizze remarked that he was emptying a barrel to fill a glass. There were mornings he went looking for Rossi just to challenge orders. Once he found the supervisor hiding in the tool shed.

"Please come out," said Fabrizze. "What kind of orders did you leave for me? Am I to take fifteen men three miles because someone thinks a rail is running? Who thinks so? Let me look into the eyes of such a man."

"What do you see?" said Rossi, giggling in a foolish way.

"Shame on you," said Fabrizze. "Shame, Rossi, shame."

"Stop it, my boy, stop it," said Rossi. "I tell you that they are slowing down a little. Do you want me to lay the men off? Stay out of sight with them. Things will be better in the spring. The men are right. You're too nervous. How do you pass the evenings?"

"I study the language," said Fabrizze. "I bought a dictionary. Every night I take a page and study it."

"You have too much energy," said Rossi. "There's nothing here for it. A dictionary, eh? I'll give you a bit of advice. Watch for a certain word. The word is girls. Stop and think."

Rossi was giggling again.

"Girls, girls," he said, pinching his foreman.

"And I came looking for you," said Fabrizze.

"But I'm serious," said Rossi. "I know the signs. Why should you bring everything to the job? Get married. Leave something home. It's time you were thinking of it."

The men were thinking of it. The fact is, they were busy making matches for Fabrizze. Before it was over he had been introduced to every daughter and niece and cousin in the area.

Gritti was one of the first with an invitation to supper. He lived on the third floor of the red rooming house and he called out when the spaghetti was on the table. The news was picked up in the hallway and passed on to the seventh floor.

"Tell Fabrizze!"

"It's on the table, Fabrizze!"

"Way, Fabrizze!"

He went downstairs.

"Sit down and eat," said Gritti. "This is my wife Nellie. I was telling you about her. I sent across the sea for her."

"Who would blame you?" said Fabrizze.

"Her father promised me everything," said Gritti. "You should see the letters he wrote. I was going to send for him. And then she came. I was looking for her baggage. Two things she brought. A Saint Christopher's medal and this crafty streak of hers. Don't be fooled, my boy. I make all the noise and she has all the power. She's taking revenge for the first years of the marriage."

"Pay no attention to him," said Nellie.

"There it is in a nutshell," said Gritti. "And now here's my daughter Mary. A worker, Fabrizze. A demon. What is it we look for in these women? I say strength and silence."

Mary was helping herself to spaghetti. She plunged her fork into the bowl. She tried to balance a meatball on the load. The meatball rolled off and she caught it in midair and popped it into her mouth. Her dark eyes were startling.

"A young man called Igino is after her," said Gritti.

"She is quick," said Fabrizze.

"He lives below us," said Gritti. "Do you hear him playing the harmonica? He plays at night under the window."

Gritti would slip from the house and catch Igino by the

back of the neck. He would squeeze and squeeze. Igino played on as the iron fingers closed tighter. Finally, he would be brought gasping to his knees.

Gritti gave a sudden demonstration of strength by squeezing Fabrizze at the calf.

"I use one hand," said Gritti. "Left or right."

"A terrible grip," said Fabrizze.

"Isn't it?" said Gritti, applying more pressure. He began to hum as though putting a song to the violence inside him.

"You stop my blood," said Fabrizze. "Igino is surely in love to keep playing under such conditions."

"It may be love," said Gritti, releasing him. "It may be that he's a musician. Who can say?"

"I'm eating more than anyone," said Mary.

"But it evens out, my darling," said Gritti. "You work harder and so you eat more. Stand up a moment for Fabrizze. Turn around. Put the fork down. All right, that's enough. It isn't right, it isn't right. Well, Fabrizze, you see how stout and solid she is? She's made for a grand effort, as they say. The girl is ambitious, I tell you. She'll drag you higher and higher. Think about her."

Later that week Cardino took Fabrizze home to have a look at Teresa. Teresa had silver bells on a bracelet and when attention drifted away she would touch her black hair and the little bells would ring. Cardino kept turning to look at her. She would be watching Fabrizze.

"Have a care," said Cardino. He was shaped like a cask for wine and it was very nearly the truth of the matter. "Have a care with my niece," he was saying. "The girl is dangerous."

46

"Who can doubt it?" said Fabrizze.

Teresa rang her little bells.

"Come into the cellar," she said. "Such golden hair you have! Your skin is like milk. And those eyes! Come along and we'll draw a bit of wine. I'm frightened of the mice down there."

"A curse on those mice," said Cardino.

Teresa took the hand of Fabrizze as though to hide him for later delight. She led him down the steep ladder stairway into the cellar. Suddenly the cellar door closed and they were alone in the winy darkness. Little bells were tinkling.

"Where is the light?" said Fabrizze.

"In those eyes," said Teresa.

"A bit of light," said Fabrizze.

Soft hands were fumbling at his throat. An arm circled his neck. Teresa whispered in a way that seemed to singe his ear.

"Light, light!" he said.

He was plucked off the ladder and given a strong sweet kiss. He struggled free. A moment later Teresa captured him and kissed even harder to make sure. He pulled away. He blundered against the barrels. Somehow he made it to the ladder. He crawled up and started to lift the door. It closed down on him. Again there was darkness and the fragrance of the girl and the little bells.

"Stay, Fabrizze, stay!" cried Cardino. "She'll show you the black bottles I buried! Wine five years old! Drink up! Hold your own with her! The house is yours! My wife went to a funeral!"

"Please open up!" said Fabrizze.

"Drink, my boy, drink!" cried Cardino. "A night to remember! A night like this and the world owes you nothing! Stay then!"

Fabrizze heard the bells. The ladder was shaking. An urgent hand closed round his left ankle. He put his back to the cellar door and lifted. He lifted Cardino who was standing on top of it. Cardino fell back against the wall. He was trying to control a glass of wine.

"Not a drop," he was saying. "I didn't lose a drop."

"Bravo," said Fabrizze.

"Tell me the truth now," said Cardino. "What do you make of the child? Speak the truth."

"She's fully grown, be sure of it," said Fabrizze.

"I admit she's a bit forward," said Cardino. "But it's only when someone strikes her fancy. It's the passion of youth, my boy. A husband will do it."

"Or two," said Fabrizze.

"Go back down a little," said Cardino. "Listen then. Do you hear the bells? I hear them all the time, I swear it!"

"I don't hear anything," said Fabrizze. "She stopped ringing."

"How innocent you are," said Cardino. "Those little bells are everywhere, my boy, and they trouble us till we die. Why is it so hard to make plans? A curse on the bells!"

The bells rang louder on the night that Bassetti took Fabrizze to visit a widow called Lena. Lena sat there in the kitchen beside a blazing coal stove. Her plump hands were on her knees. She kept her piercing black eyes on

Fabrizze. He broke into a sweat. He looked from Lena to the stove. He turned to Bassetti for help.

Bassetti spoke at length of his wit and power and prospects. He went on to tell a story about a railroad foreman who returned to Italy. Suddenly Lena left the kitchen. Returning, she made a sign for Bassetti to continue. Water was running somewhere in the house.

"He lived alone," said Bassetti. "It's a bad thing."

"A terrible thing," said Lena.

"I know what it is to be alone," said Bassetti. "I've been alone for thirty years."

"Poor soul," said Lena.

"This foreman would forget things," said Bassetti. "One day he wanted to fix some ties on the main line. He had a special way of doing it. His men lifted the track and held it there. Out came the old ties and in went the new. The other men were tamping."

"Good, good," said Lena. "Isn't it?"

"It was bad," said Bassetti. "The rail kicked out in the heat. Like an elbow. And here the train was coming. He forgot it."

"Isn't it exciting?" said Lena, to Fabrizze.

"He went to flag the train," said Bassetti.

"He forgot the flag," said Fabrizze.

"He remembered the flag," said Bassetti. "But it was too late. The train was wrecked. And no one could find him. And the next thing we heard he was back in Italy."

"What more can you say?" said Lena.

"But I hear water running," said Bassetti.

49

"This Fabrizze will bring lovely children, eh?" said Lena.

One of her hands was now resting on his knee.

"I'm filling the tub for you," she said. "A hot bath."

Bassetti rescued him.

After two months of this Fabrizze felt sure that Grace Mendone was the only girl he had missed on his round of the neighborhood. He was wrong. Rossi extended an invitation.

"A double surprise," said Rossi. "First a fine supper for you. I prepared it myself before coming to work. A real delicacy. You must eat nothing all day. And then after supper there'll be dessert, eh? Your heart will flutter."

"My heart will flutter?" said Fabrizze, going numb.

"My godchild is coming for you," said Rossi. "But why do you look the other way? You've heard of her! What a shy one you are! She's called Carrie. I'm told she can take fifty-pound sacks of flour under each arm."

"Take them where?" said Fabrizze, glumly.

"Where they do the most good!" said Rossi. "She's a girl of excellent judgment!"

"She's coming for me," said Fabrizze.

He went to the house of his supervisor. He sat in the chair opposite the big black stove.

"I sent my Nancy away," said Rossi. "It's a supper just for the two of us. Guess what we have. Take a little guess. What do you smell?"

"Vinegar," said Fabrizze.

"Forget that," said Rossi. "She roasted vinegar peppers with rice and honey. There's something else. Guess, guess."

"Veal breast?"

"Never mind," said Rossi. "Wait, wait."

The kitchen was hot. They drank glass after glass of wine. Fabrizze watched the stove. It began to fascinate him. The wine went straight to his head. He was watching the stove as though something would spring forth into his lap.

"I have plans for you," said Rossi. "I'm going to make you my assistant and break you in on my job. You'll be the supervisor when I move into the office. Nothing will stop you, my boy. You have imagination. The fools have been showing you their daughters. You know what's happened? All their wives are crazy for you. They come down with colds and coughs and fevers. It's an epidemic! One of them was hearing your name in her sleep. She was saying it!"

"Please, Rossi, please."

"I hear that one of them wanted to give you a bath! Admit it! What a triumph! I'm glad I sent my Nancy away! Why should I make her nervous with you?"

The time had come.

"Are you ready to eat?" said Rossi.

"But I'm starved," said Fabrizze.

"Are you really hungry? Speak, speak!"

"Put it on the table!" said Fabrizze.

Rossi jumped up and whipped open the stove. Inside was a pan dark and long—with eels! Great black eels were watching each other! They were watching Rossi! They turned on Fabrizze!

He dropped his glass. A cry escaped him as he made for the door. He fell down the stairs.

So ended his round of visits.

AND yet the bells went on ringing. The search for love filled him with longing for it. He thought of Grace Mendone. How eager he was to meet her. Her presence in the neighborhood was like an invitation coaxing him clear of the other girls. He questioned his men. They had started a fire in him and so they kept it burning.

"Grace came across the street," said Rumbone. "All the way across just to say good morning."

"It's like a dance when she moves," said Penza.

Rumbone held up his hands to frame a picture of the girl dancing down on him in the sunlight. Fabrizze was in the picture, too. He was there listening to every word.

"Those eyes were on me," said Rumbone. "I saw lights of gold. I couldn't think of anything to say. Not one word. I cleared my throat. She smiled to encourage me. I was wringing my hands."

"It happened to me," said Penza.

"I was getting sick inside," said Rumbone. "And then the words came. I spoke right out. I asked her to marry me."

"Good for you," said Penza. "And then?"

"She leaned over," said Rumbone. "She came closer and

closer. Her hair brushed my cheek. Like a kiss. She whispered in my ear. So soft it was. Like a kiss. Like this."

Rumbone leaned over to whisper to Penza.

"What is it?" said Fabrizze. "What was it?"

"Come closer then," said Rumbone. "So soft it was. How did she say it? 'It's almost enough,' she said. 'It's almost enough that you come from the Abruzzi,' she said."

"Back to work," said Fabrizze.

"They say she sings in the house," said Penza.

"She sings to her grandfather," said Rumbone. "She'll sing to you and your children, Fabrizze, if given the chance."

"So be it," said Fabrizze. "I'm for it."

"I'll take you to meet her," said Rumbone.

"We'll be uneasy there," said Fabrizze. "I've seen it in the past weeks. I have a plan."

"Lose no time," said Penza. "A proposal was made."

Fabrizze was ready to make one. The truth is, he had fallen in love. He decided it was time to meet the girl.

He took to walking two blocks out of his way just to pass her house on Jackson Street. Day after day he rushed by holding his breath. Nothing happened. He could bear it no longer. One spring morning he resolved to go round and round the block until dark. It was on his third trip that the upstairs window opened. His heart skipped a beat. Suddenly she was there calling to him.

"Good morning to you," she said.

"Good morning, good morning," said Fabrizze.

"Are you going around again?" she said. "I just saw you."

"I was looking for someone," said Fabrizze.

"Can I help you? Who is it?"

"I was looking for you," said Fabrizze.

"My name is Grace Mendone."

"But I recognized you. I am Cennino Fabrizze. I work for the railroad. And I gather information about you."

"About me?"

"Everyone tells me things. It's like gathering flowers. You have friends on every side."

"They tell you about me?" said Grace. "But why?"

"Because I ask them."

"And what do they say?"

"Some say this and some say that. But they all say that Grace Mendone is good to be with. So good to be with that a proposal has been made."

"Thank you."

"It's what they say."

"And they speak of you," said Grace. "May I ask you something? Is there work on the railroad for my grandfather?"

"Can he do it?"

"He is good company," said Grace.

"Can I talk with him?"

"He works three days a week in the market. Do you have time to come and visit us tonight?"

"I'll be here early."

"We'll be waiting."

"I'll be waiting longer," said Fabrizze.

It was a splendid evening.

Mendone never once stopped talking. His bald head was aglow and his fine white moustache followed the joyous curve of his mouth. Fabrizze listened to the sing-song of talk and watched Grace out of the corner of his eye. Her pale dark beauty struck him speechless. Suddenly he was afraid to turn and look at her. He leaned forward in his chair and fixed his glance on Mendone. The old man was delighted and drew his own chair closer.

"It's years ago I came to America," said Mendone. "I had a taste for money and power and corn meal. The corn meal was for balance. My brother took me aside before I left. 'Your appetites change now that you change countries?' he said. 'No, no,' I told him. 'I'm changing countries because of my appetites.' 'You aim low,' he said. 'Why not put in strength of character as a thing to strive for?' 'Very good,' I said. 'From this moment I put in strength of character, and take out the corn meal.' It was all a dream, Fabrizze, except for the corn meal."

"He is here to see you about work," said Grace.

"I clean vegetables in the market," said Mendone. "Lettuce and carrots and cabbage. I'm good for nothing else."

"Shame on you," said Grace.

Fabrizze blushed in delight.

"It's a strange thing," said Mendone. "In Italy I was as sure of my talents as of the fact there were no opportunities. I came here. Now I'm as sure of the opportunities as of the fact I have no talents. I sit in the sun with a cabbage in my hands. What do you make of it?"

"It's nonsense," said Grace. "You were too old when you came."

"I lived alone for a time," said Mendone. "I managed to put a little money on this house. And then I sent for the girl. Her mother is dead, and my son married again."

"I believe there's a job for you," said Fabrizze.

"Such an old man?"

"One of the men was over seventy," said Fabrizze. "His name is Bassetti and he just left off a few weeks ago. I can put you on as my assistant for a while."

"You mean until they find out," said Mendone. "Really though, it's kind of you. Let me tell you how happy I am that you are here. And the girl is happier still. Why? Because you came to see me about the work."

"But he did," said Grace.

"Which of us is the fool here?" said Mendone. "Let it rest then. Stay a little, my boy. Mancini is coming downstairs for a game of cards. Pass the evening with us."

"I'll be here until you send me away," said Fabrizze.

He made three visits a week during the next month. Mancini was always there. The carpenter had black eyes and a mop of black hair splashed with gray. He was suspicious the first time he saw Fabrizze. He drank more wine than anyone and he played every card like a trump.

"A man called Gritti works with me," said Fabrizze. "Is it true you came from Sicily with him?"

"He came with me!" said Mancini, playing a trump. "Gritti can't put a nail in the wall! I wouldn't trust him with a nail!"

"There's a man called Cardino," said Fabrizze. "He speaks of your ability. He showed me the cabinet you made for him."

"Cardino can't put a nail!" said Mancini. "Not even a nail!"

The carpenter knew that he was in trouble. Night after night he found himself watching for Fabrizze as for a thief. He came down from his room whenever the front door opened or closed.

"Where is he?" Mancini would say, as though Grace was hiding him somewhere. "Where did he go?"

"He'll come tomorrow," said Grace.

"Who came in then?"

"My grandfather went out."

"Why isn't he here?" said Mancini. "Why does he come every other day? Why not every day? Why is he hiding in between?"

The next day Fabrizze arrived just before dark. Grace had set aside a bit of supper for him. A sudden hush fell over the house. Light was fading. Mancini sat there with his head resting on his hand. He sipped wine and watched for a false move. He could make nothing of the conversation.

"These potatoes are very good," said Fabrizze.

"I roasted them in olive oil," said Grace. "With parsley."

"My grandmother used to steam them," said Fabrizze. "They were the red potatoes."

"She steamed them?" said Grace.

"She left the skins on," said Fabrizze. "She covered them with a damp cloth. A very low fire. We had to wait and wait for them. But how sweet they were. I make them here and they have a different taste. Now I remember how they were."

"It depends where you are," said Grace, softly.

"It depends who is with you," said Fabrizze.

"Potatoes are potatoes," said Mancini. "And why is everyone speaking so softly? It's like a church in here!"

The card game started. Mancini was watching Grace and Fabrizze. Long breathless looks filled him with desperation. Often he flung up his cards and plunged into the basement where he set about hammering and sawing and singing at the top of his voice. One night he left the table and a moment later something fell down the stairs and pounded the floor. Everyone jumped up.

"Mancini!" said Grace.

Mancini gave a cry terrible with triumph. He had gone up to his room and thrown a chair all the way down the stairs.

"Come here," he said, hurrying down. "Look at this chair. I made it with my own hands. No nails, no nails. I myself chose the wood. Feel it, Fabrizze, feel it! Nothing loose! Like a tree!"

He lifted the chair and for an instant it seemed he would throw it through the window. He carried it to his room and then came down. He went right to the cupboard. He embraced and shook it until the dishes rattled.

"It's hanging by a thread!" he said, glancing back over his shoulder. "It was a shoemaker put this up!"

He came over and pounded the corner of the kitchen table.

"This is the leg I fixed!" he said. His burning black eyes held Fabrizze. "Quick, turn the table over!"

He swept off the cards and turned the table on its top.

"You, Fabrizze, you," he said. "Do you see how I fixed

it? Try to loosen the leg. Tear this leg off and you'll tear the table to pieces! How solid and strong!"

"A fine piece of work," said Fabrizze. "You put the rest of the table to shame."

"I changed it," said Mancini. "I tapered it. Follow the leg with your eye. You see how it goes up to join the top?"

"But it flows up," said Fabrizze. "And then it's gone."

"It flows, it flows!" cried Mancini. "A work of magic! But I'll fix this house from cellar to chimney if they give me the chance! Quick, turn the table up!"

"I'm putting my glass down," said Mendone.

Mancini was pounding with pride.

And yet all was lost for him.

Late on a warm windy night the men were drinking and playing cards. Grace watched the game. The look of Mancini worried her. It seemed there was no release of the tension in him. After each game he insisted on plunging into another. He won again and again. He kept drinking.

Grace went out to the porch swing. She sat there swinging. Now and again came a loving rush of wind. The leaves of maple and sycamore were wild with kissing in the sweet spring darkness.

Fabrizze was overwhelmed with love for her. No longer could he keep his mind on the game.

"It's your play," said Mendone. "Wrong again, my boy. I take with the king and play the ace. I sip wine. I play another ace. I sip more wine. And now Mancini loses his queen."

Mancini slammed his queen down. The table wobbled.

59

"Did you see it?" he said. He was filled with exultance and power. "It hardly stands! Everything depends on my leg! I tell you, Mendone, this leg will stand for a thousand years!"

"It will stand alone," said Mendone.

"It's like a pillar!" said Mancini, pounding the table again and again. "I poured my strength into it! Give me a free hand in this place! Everything is ruined! Look at the cupboard! All the floors creak! The ceiling cracks and buckles! The foundation is sinking! Even the porch swing cries out! Listen, listen!"

"A bit of paint," said Mendone.

"What a fool you are!"

"A bit of faith," said Mendone, gravely.

"You need a master hand!" cried Mancini, springing on the table. He jumped up and down. "Give me one year and I'll make a palace of it! Say the word! I'll fix everything!"

There was silence.

Mancini glanced out the window. Grace was watching him. The secret glowing look of her gripped his heart. So far away she was. His eyes filled with tears. He lost her in the night. His powerful hands came together in a convulsive way. In a moment he was fumbling for his red handkerchief. He wiped his face.

"Come down then," said Mendone, gently.

"It's quiet again," said Mancini.

"Give me your hand," said Mendone.

Mancini started to lose his balance. Fabrizze steadied him and helped him down. The floor creaked beneath him.

"Did you hear?" said Mancini.

"Come along then," said Mendone.

Mancini turned and bowed slightly to Fabrizze.

"Good night," he said, trying to smile. "The queen is lost, and she is won, eh? Good night to you."

Mendone led him up the creaking stairs.

"Listen, listen," said Mancini.

"A bit of sleep," said Mendone.

"Everything," said Mancini. "Everything but the heart."

Fabrizze sat there in the kitchen. All strength had drained from him. He drank another glass of wine. After a while he went out to say good night.

"Stay a little," said Grace. "Is it so late?"

"This Mancini is a good man."

"A fine man," said Grace. "But he knew I couldn't marry him. He knew it before you came."

"I'm weak and dizzy."

"It's the wine," said Grace.

"A thing stronger than wine."

Grace was swinging. Her eyes were lowered. For a moment she was absorbed like a child in her own living beauty.

Talk and laughter filled the porches of the street. A sweet forlorn harmonica was heard. Suddenly a boy came flashing by on his bicycle. His hands were straight up and his feet were fixed on the handlebars. He was laughing.

"You'll fall," said a girl. "You really will. I'm going in."

The boy carried laughter down the aisle of tossing trees.

"Come and sit here," said Grace. "Sit beside me."

Fabrizze was trembling. He took aim and somehow

made it to the swing. He sat in the corner away from her.

Grace took three quick steps to start the swing again. She drew her legs up. The swing dragged to a stop.

"Don't you like to swing?" she said.

"I do, I do," said Fabrizze.

"You must lift your feet," she said.

"I'll do it," said Fabrizze. "I'll do it."

Soon they were swinging together in the dark. The swing kept on soaring. Fabrizze held on for dear life. His head was spinning. The night was a blur of dark and silver and the whispering leaves.

"What are you thinking?" said Grace.

The swing slowed.

"Tell me," said Grace. "Tell me."

"If only I could," said Fabrizze. "It's your hair, too."

"My hair?"

"You never take it down. I never saw it."

"I'll take it down," she said. "For you."

She turned. Her pale beauty was hidden away. Her fingers were quick and sure in the dark. Suddenly the breath-taking mass of hair tumbled beneath her shoulders.

Fabrizze melted back.

"Do you want to touch it?" said Grace, softly.

Fabrizze watched her.

"Touch it," she whispered. "Touch it then."

The black sweet hair sent shivers through him.

Grace turned into his arms and he was kissing her warm lips.

IV

THEY were married.

It was during the celebration that Rossi announced the promotion of Fabrizze to acting supervisor of the railroad yard.

"There you have it," said Penza. "They were telling me that Fabrizze needed a wife. He married the most beautiful girl in the city. They were telling me he was too young to be a foreman. Now he's the supervisor. They were telling me I had a hole in my shoe. Now I have a hole in the other shoe."

Summer was keeping the promises of spring. The long days were rich with joy and love. An air of triumph like

63

music filled the house on Jackson Street. It swelled forth to quicken every hope in the neighborhood. Friends came with words of advice and wisdom for the young couple. No secret was withheld. Everyone took an interest in their happiness and so shared in it. Cardino remarked that Grace and Fabrizze had put each other under a spell, and the neighborhood, watching close, fell under it.

For a while Mendone fell under. He started work as a special assistant on the railroad. For weeks he was eating dried figs and nuts. He heard from Rumbone that such a diet had restored vitality to a man of ninety. With his first pay he bought an old violin from a peddler who promised to give him three lessons. The peddler returned to sell him a stool where he could sit if he played the harp or piano. He spoke of sending across the sea for a wife.

"It's an idea," he said, tapping his pipe on the porch. "It's a good sign to have this idea at my age."

"I agree," said Grace. She sat beside Fabrizze on the swing.

"A man in our village was a father at eighty," said Fabrizze.

"Who told him so?" said Mendone.

"It's true," said Fabrizze. "You should see him. Eyes bright as fire. One tooth missing. He fell off a roof and knocked out a front tooth. He used to shake his fist at that roof when he passed it. What an appetite he had."

"For what?" said Grace, smiling in anticipation.

"Figs and nuts," said Fabrizze. "Nuts and figs."

"I chew and chew these figs," said Mendone. "My jaw aches with them. I crack and crack these nuts. I pick and pick at them. I think it's a way to pass the time, and nothing more. . . . Be sure to wake me for work."

Grace would be at the window when they left the house.

"Hello, Fabrizze, hello," someone called.

"Hello, hello," said Fabrizze.

Nellie was shaking her carpet.

"Look who's there," she said.

"Look who's there," said Fabrizze.

"It's Fabrizze," said Bassetti. "And the special assistant."

"Grace is waiting," said Fabrizze. "The coffee is hot."

Suddenly they were gone round the corner. The street had come alive with talk and laughter.

For three months Mendone led Fabrizze in and followed him out of the railroad yard. The old man was first to arrive in the morning and last to leave at night. In this way he made sure that nothing happened.

"He comes to take lunch with Fabrizze," said Rossi.

"He likes to be in the fresh air," said Penza.

"It's the trains," said Rumbone. "It's the excitement of the trains bringing him back."

Fabrizze advised Mendone to pay no attention to them.

"They need tools and I need weapons," said Fabrizze. "You're like a weapon. Keep lighting the pipe and watching them through the smoke. Here is a pair of white gloves. Wear them all day. Follow me. Sometimes I make mistakes. You'll be the one to point them out."

"Really?"

"I'll warn you beforehand," said Fabrizze.

For three months it went well. Grace washed the white gloves and they could be seen hanging in the sunlight.

She listened in the evening to little talks on the effect of power. Mendone concluded that power was as nourishing as it was delicious. He went downtown to have his picture taken.

One summer afternoon Fabrizze sent him to fetch the water boy Poggio. Poggio had been gone since morning. The men were grading under a white and terrible sun. Rails were smoking in the heat.

"Poggio will wear that bucket when I see him," said Cardino.

"Is it rest he wants?" said Gritti. "I make a place for him."

The idea took hold. Ominous words echoed down the line.

"Down he goes."

"All the lies and laughter."

"Goodbye, Poggio, goodbye."

Fabrizze called Mendone aside.

"Find the boy and bring water," said Fabrizze. "These men are choking with thirst. Listen to them. It's getting worse."

"He brought no water at all?" said Mendone.

"I don't understand it," said Fabrizze. "Two buckets of water, I told him, and nothing more is expected of you. Not even one will he bring. And still he comes every morning for the bucket."

Mendone set forth.

He walked half a mile in the sun. He went astray in a patch of woods. He staggered into the clear again and up the last long hill.

Poggio was napping under a maple tree. He lay there in his underwear. His bare feet were cool in the bubbling stream and his head was pillowed sweetly in his palms.

"It's the end, my boy, it's the end," said Mendone, after he caught his breath. "It's all up with you."

"Mendone!"

"It is Mendone. Mendone caught you in the act."

"Off with your shoes, Foreman Mendone," said Poggio. "How good it is to see you."

"It's the worst thing that could happen to you."

"Sit in the shade a little," said Poggio. "Rest yourself."

"Never mind, never mind," said Mendone. "The men are dropping with thirst and you sleep in the shade here. And with your feet in their water. You go too far with it."

"But it's not the same water, Foreman Mendone. See how it runs. Fresh every second. Fresh since you spoke. That's the wonder of it. Stay a while. We'll go back with a full cold bucket. I had a cramp in the stomach. Look how my tongue is green."

"The truth is, I'm worn out," said Mendone.

"It's the heat," said Poggio. "And all this talk, too. Sit a moment then. It's a long walk."

Mendone slipped off his shoes and socks. He soaked his aching feet in the stream. He kept looking over his shoulder.

"A secret chill is in it," Poggio was saying.

"Guilt," said Mendone.

"It will reduce the swelling," said Poggio.

"What swelling? Where do you see it?"

67

"It's thrilling," said Poggio. "Off with your gloves. Put your hands in. It flows right through you."

"Very nice, my boy, very nice," said Mendone, splashing his face and hair. "Tell me something. Seriously, eh? Did I frighten you when I crept up?"

"It was an awful fright, Foreman Mendone. Your name itself was enough. It's like the gong of doom."

"The gong of doom," said Mendone.

"Mendone, Mendone," said Poggio.

"We must be going," said Mendone.

"I had to lie down a little," said Poggio.

They dozed in the shade.

Far off there was a stricken cry.

"What's that?" said Poggio, sitting up.

"Where, where?" said Mendone.

"Some poor man—look on the hill!"

A chain of hands took hold along the crest of the hill. Dark figures loomed above. For a moment they were frozen high in the misty white light. A cry packed with revenge split the air. Suddenly the black wave of men came sweeping down. They were armed with picks and shovels.

"He's mine!" someone cried.

"Mine, mine!"

"Run, Mendone, run!" said Poggio. "A beast is loose!"

"Poor me, poor me!"

"Give me your hand! Come this way!"

They managed an escape as their pursuers flung themselves into the stream. Fabrizze salvaged the shoes and brought them home.

68

"And the gloves?" said Mendone.

"The men buried them under the tree," said Fabrizze. "Along with Poggio's cap. It was a little ceremony. They gave me a look near the end of it."

MENDONE was merely the first in a procession of workers hired by Fabrizze. Appeals were coming from every side. It happened to be a busy time on the railroad and so he was given a free hand in the hiring. He refused no one. Word of his kindness carried into immigrant settlements throughout the city. Men seeking work came right to the house. One afternoon he found a stranger waiting on the porch swing.

"Come inside," said Fabrizze. "A glass of wine."

"Your lovely wife brought wine. It's too warm in there."

"I'll wash up and be with you in a moment."

"Take your time, Supervisor. How young you are!"

Fabrizze went inside. A man was sipping wine in the kitchen.

"This is Russo," said Grace. "He came for work."

"The work is heavy," said Fabrizze. "Very heavy."

"So much the better," said Russo. "Don't be fooled by my size. Look at these hands. I'm a farmer."

"The job is yours," said Fabrizze. "I myself was a farmer."

"Benedico," said Russo, blessing him.

"One thing about a farmer," said Fabrizze. "He takes out only what he puts in. Or less."

"Cardino was right about you," said Russo. "Did he speak of me? He's my cumpare."

"I was watching for you," said Fabrizze.

There was a burst of laughter from the porch. The man was swinging out there and flirting with women in the street. Higher and higher he went. How gay he was!

"A cumpare of mine," said Russo.

"You're surrounded," said Fabrizze. "And so am I."

It was true. Each of his men on the railroad had introduced at least one cumpare. Cumpare no longer meant godfather. A cumpare was a needy friend located between a cumpare who would help him and a cumpare looking to him for help.

"I have a cumpare," said Gritti, one day.

"What can we do for him?" said Fabrizze.

"He plays the clarinet," said Gritti.

"Tell him to come to work," said Fabrizze. "He'll play for the men during the lunch hour."

"I thought of it," said Gritti. "Wait until you hear him play. His wife says he saves himself for it."

"But he must work before and after lunch," said Fabrizze.

"He makes his own songs," said Gritti. "He's like this Igino. Think of it. He makes songs out of his head."

"Still, he must work a little," said Fabrizze.

"I was expecting it," said Gritti. "I'll tell him."

"It's only for work that we give money," said Fabrizze. "But we'll value him for his music."

70

News of his promotion to supervisor had reached Rivisondoli. A long letter came from Augustine. He announced that he had married the mother of his son. He went on to say that the entire village was rejoicing in the success of Fabrizze. Indeed, the account of it given by Rumbone had started a wave of unrest. Augustine sent a list of friends who were suddenly determined to come to America. He offered to lend part of the passage money if Fabrizze would help them to get settled. There were several women in need of husbands. Augustine swore it was so and he enclosed their pictures.

"We have three empty rooms," said Grace. "They can stay with us until they get started."

Fabrizze went ahead with it.

He wrote a letter telling of life in the New World. He tried to be honest and yet every word was informed with love and shining hope. It was an invitation to the feast. Augustine read the letter to a gathering of men in the square; and then he took up his adroit position beside the community oven, where women brought their bread to be baked.

More pictures came to Fabrizze. He sent money to those bent on leaving at once and he promised to have work waiting when they arrived. Along with Mendone he went the rounds of the neighborhood in search of prospective husbands and wives. One night he stayed home and made a match for Mancini.

"I told her about you," said Fabrizze. "She's writing a letter with the help of Augustine. Look at her picture."

"I won't do it," said Mancini. "Leave me alone, Fabrizze."

"But you are alone," said Fabrizze.

"Don't get me all upset," said Mancini. "Night after night I leave this kitchen drunk with wine and words."

"Tell us her name," said Mendone. "I beg of you."

"She's called Lucia," said Fabrizze.

"Lucia," said Mendone, sighing. "Lucia, Lucia. I think of the sea and the moon. Drink to Lucia."

"Lucia, eh?" said Mancini.

"Look, look," said Fabrizze. "Wait a moment then. Mendone is impartial here. We'll see what he makes of her."

"Such a lovely color," said Mendone.

"It's the high color of the mountain people," said Fabrizze.

"Look at these arms," said Mendone. "Here is a girl to clear the way for someone."

"How she gazes into my eyes," said Fabrizze. "Now I remember this Lucia. All week she worked in the house. Sunday she took a bit of sun. No more than a bit of sun on the front step. Like a flower. Your time has come, Mancini."

"Let me see her then," said Mancini. "Good to look at, God bless her! And youthful, too.... What's this? Look how her arms and legs are crossed. Look, look!"

"How he strikes to the heart of it," said Fabrizze.

"But she's all in a knot," said Mancini. "It's nerves!"

"No better than a thief," said Fabrizze. "One glance and he steals the secret."

"What secret?" said Mancini. "What is it?"

72

"Tell us the secret," said Mendone. "Out with it."

"He'll tell it as soon as he thinks of it," said Grace.

"I have it," said Fabrizze. "Why is she in a knot? Think of the bride. Are you thinking? Do you see the bride? She's wearing white and she's blushing. Why is it? She's in between, my friend. She looks back and she looks forward. It's the last morning of her innocence, eh? How sad! But she looks forward to the night of love. How wonderful! Back and forth. It makes her nervous. Look at Lucia. She's holding in all the passion. Innocence wins the day! What a struggle!"

"Bravo, bravo," said Mendone.

"She's waiting," said Fabrizze. "She's waiting for love!"

"You're sure she's waiting," said Mancini.

"Passion, passion," said Mendone. "I empty my glass to it."

"Passion, eh?" said Mancini. "I know all about it. Passion and nothing more. It's always the same story with these women. Tell me what her father offers."

"I'm struck dumb," said Fabrizze. "My eyes play tricks on me. Isn't her cheek like the rose? What about this brown hair? Look into these eyes. How deep and blue! Follow the curve of her mouth. Ripe and sweet as a plum. This girl belongs in a vault. Wait, Mancini, wait. She speaks for herself. Listen, listen. I remember her voice. I tell you I heard it again! Just now!"

"I believe it," said Mancini. "You see things and you hear things. What did she say?"

"She said yes to you," said Fabrizze. "Yes and yes and yes!"

"The picture makes me warm inside," said Mendone. "The girl is like a furnace."

"Let me see her again," said Mancini. "Before you start on the birthmarks. One more look."

"One last look," said Fabrizze. "Really, you take more than a fair share. Let me tell you another secret."

"I rub my hands by the warmth of her," said Mendone.

"A surprise," said Fabrizze.

"Out with it," said Grace, laughing.

"Are you listening?" said Fabrizze. "Augustine put a star on the back of the picture. Look here. This girl is someone special. You'll treat her well, eh? Rain on the roof."

"Give me the picture," said Mancini. "Who can think straight in this kitchen? I'll study it in my room a little. I'll see how she looks at different times of day."

"Never, never," said Fabrizze. "It isn't right for her picture to be in your room. Say the word and she's yours. I'll tell her to come at once. I'll even send the fare. If you're not satisfied, I'll be responsible for her."

"Or I," said Mendone.

"My next stop is Rumbone," said Fabrizze. "He can't put a nail in the wall, but one look will be enough for him. And then there's Penza. Make up your mind. Rain on the roof."

"What rain?" said Mancini. "What's happening?"

"Think a moment," said Fabrizze. "Remember last night when it rained? You were up at three with it. You were sawing boards and singing to keep up your courage. The rain was everywhere. Where were you? Alone in your room. Get married, my friend. You'll wait for the rain on the roof. You'll be alone. You'll be alone with love and beauty."

"My head is spinning!" said Mancini. "Write the girl, write the girl! You made it up in your head! Write then! It's you sending the fare!"

"A furnace," said Mendone. "Open the windows."

"I'll write tonight," said Fabrizze. "I'll send your love!"

"Send it then!" cried Mancini. "And see that her father sends something! And never mind with the sheets and pillow cases!"

It was easier to arrange tentative matches for the men coming from Italy. Grace and Fabrizze would go over the list and make sure that boy and girl suited each other with respect to age and temperament. They would settle on a likely pair. Fabrizze sent Mendone to alert the prospect.

"I spoke with Fabrizze," Mendone would say. "He's excited."

"He's always excited," said Cardino.

"He has just the right husband for Teresa."

"Don't say it!" said Cardino, in delight. "But I saw him on the job and he said nothing."

"I spoke too soon," said Mendone. "Perhaps he changed his mind about it. Such care he takes."

Several days later Fabrizze turned up at the house. He sat across from Cardino at the kitchen table. Cardino put his glass down and leaned forward. He had the curious look of one not so much hearing as overhearing.

"Is it what I think, Supervisor?" he said.

Fabrizze was absorbed in a series of pictures. He studied

each one of them. Now and then there was a flash of interest in his face. Once he gave a little chuckle. A moment later he was grave and troubled. Cardino was beginning to think Fabrizze should have his picture taken.

"Don't say it!" said Cardino, seeing him smile.

Fabrizze put aside all but one of the pictures.

"Teresa," he said. "Look here a moment. Do you find such a man attractive? He's called Lorenzo."

"I knew it would be someone nice," said Teresa.

"Into the other room with you," said Cardino.

"Let me see the picture," said his wife Adriana.

"Into the other room with you," said Cardino.

The women disappeared.

"I see you're in control here," said Fabrizze.

"It means nothing," said Cardino. "They show a little respect because they like you. I'll have to pay for it. They'll cut me to pieces after you go."

"Will you look at the picture?" said Fabrizze.

"Let me have it," said Cardino. "Lorenzo, Lorenzo. Benedico! He sits on the chair like it's a horse on parade. But why isn't he smiling a little? How he stares. He looks right through me. He's found me out, the scoundrel!"

"Bright eyes, bright eyes," said Fabrizze.

"A wild look," said Cardino. "His cork is too tight."

"The man is determined," said Fabrizze.

"But he's a bit small," said Cardino. "Speak the truth, my boy. His shoes don't reach the floor. He's undersize."

"I admit Lorenzo is no giant," said Fabrizze. "But he's sweet of nature. And resolute."

"Resolute?"

"They tell a story about him," said Fabrizze. "At the crack of dawn he throws off the bedcovers. He stands to the day like a cannon."

"A small cannon," said Cardino.

"You mix it up," said Fabrizze. "Size has nothing to do with it. Look how much juice is in the grape."

"I'm to send the fare, is that it?" said Cardino.

"I'll send the money," said Fabrizze. "Let me show my faith in this man. I'll put him to work, too. If Teresa has no feeling for him, she needn't marry him. She'll find another and so will he. But I remind you Lorenzo is a demon with shovel or axe. He'll chop down a tree before you're out from under it. Like a cannon."

"Who can keep up with this?" said Cardino. "You get me climbing and leave me on the ledge. Let it rest then. We'll talk on Sunday. Do you know I start for church in the morning and never get past your house? . . . Take another glass before you leave me."

"Is it true you're selling the wine?"

"I'm beginning again," said Cardino. "Last night I decided to sell three glasses to Rumbone. It was after he drank them. We had an argument. 'Who told you I was a customer?' he said. In the end I went to the rooming house and bought the three glasses back."

"Give me another glass," said Fabrizze. "Let me spend."

"Spend your time and it's enough."

"Mendone talks of selling wine."

"Sell coffee," said Cardino. "Your kitchen is always full."

So it was.

All week people were coming in and out of the house on

77

Jackson Street. Recent arrivals in the country would be seeking advice and work from the supervisor with the golden hair. Some asked for temporary lodging. Neighbors fell into a round of regular visits. The widowed sisters Adelina and Josephine came twice a week. Their faces were like old brown shoes. Adelina told fortunes. How dark and dangerous was the future! Josephine sipped coffee from a saucer and yearned for the past.

"Listen, listen," said Mancini. "I'm bringing the news. Today is Friday. The sun is shining on all your trouble."

"It's the clever carpenter, eh?" said Adelina.

"Get married, you fool," said Josephine.

Friends came to have their letters written and read. Every month without fail Gritti brought a long letter of appeal from his mother in Sicily. They set his head aching.

"Your brother had the dizzy spell," his mother would say. "All was going black. He failed to work again. Little enough there is. You were always the stronger of the two. His son Carlo never seems to grow. He is no higher than the table, poor child. Some say he will shoot up all at once. Others say it is lack of meat. He has a dimple in his chin. Such sad eyes! The picture of you. But with none of your strength. Truly, the crop will be ruined with all this sun. The cow is sinking fast."

It would have come as no surprise to hear that the island was sinking into the sea.

"Write, Fabrizze, write," said Gritti. "My mother has these ideas about America. You must tell her how things are."

"And how are they?" said Fabrizze.

78

"You see how they are," said Gritti, in a sullen way.

"Good."

"Look again."

"Your family is well," said Fabrizze. "You seem to be happy on the job. You're getting the feel of this country. You even learn the language a little."

"All from my daughter," said Gritti. "Is it good to have your children tell you things?"

"But you are taking hold here," said Fabrizze. "They'll never shake you loose."

"Am I any younger?" said Gritti.

"Is this news to your mother?" said Grace.

"Enough, enough," said Gritti. "Send five dollars. We'll make the letter next week. The truth is, nothing happened."

"It's for you to look again," said Fabrizze.

Saturday was the most pleasant time of all.

Bassetti came in the evening with a basket of dandelions or mushrooms. On occasion the old man would simply gather wildflowers for Grace. He called out when he reached the house and then he climbed one step at a time. A sprig of mint was behind his ear and in the pocket of his shirt. Grace would set his chair beside the window. He nibbled grapes and ate the ripest banana. He dipped hard little crusts of bread in red wine.

"Here is a man older than prayer," said Mendone.

Fabrizze had once complained of a stiff neck and so Bassetti came every week to massage him. Fabrizze removed his shirt and sat in the kitchen. Bassetti lit his pipe.

79

Presently he was working his warm fingers into the neck and shoulders of the supervisor.

"My muscles begin to tighten on Thursday," said Fabrizze. "I look forward to your visit."

"I'm sure it helps you," said Bassetti. "If nothing else, my boy, it opens the passages. It frees the passages between the heart and the brain."

"If nothing else?" said Fabrizze. "Did you hear him? The heart will tell the brain, and the brain will tell the heart."

"Benedico," said Mendone. "A new man is here."

Bassetti puffed his pipe and worked his fingers. Fabrizze made soft sounds of pleasure.

"Ah," he said.

"Ah," said Bassetti, knowingly. "Hold still then, my boy. I'm loosening my fingers for Mendone. There's work with him."

"You'll be here all night," said Mendone.

"I had this feeling when I came in," said Bassetti. "I may be wrong. Is it true that Grace will have a child?"

"How did you know?" said Grace. "We just found out."

"I see something in your eyes," said Bassetti.

"And in mine?" said Mendone. "What do you see in mine?"

"A craving," said Bassetti.

"A craving?" said Mendone. "A craving for what?"

"Everything beyond your need," said Bassetti.

A late soft breeze lifted the curtain. Grace sat there sewing in the corner. She was thinking of her child. Mendone sipped wine and filled the glasses again. Bassetti reached

80

for his and kept massaging with the other hand. Secretly, Fabrizze slipped a dollar into his pocket.

"I'll tell you what happened to me," said Bassetti.

"Nothing happened to you," said Mendone. "You're too old."

"Listen then," said Bassetti. "It was a few weeks ago. I was getting ready for bed when I had this pain in the heart. It pinched me and then it went away. The skin of my face was tight and cold. I began to sweat. It was a warning. It would be finished for me in the night. I drank a glass of wine and straightened the room. I went to bed. I lay there thinking of my wife and my mother. And then I was thinking of everyone. And then I fell asleep."

"Wine and sleep," said Mendone. "Just what you needed."

"Never will I forget the next morning," said Bassetti. "I saw everything for the first time. How can I say it? It was like a welcome for a guest. It was perfect. There was the sun with its light and warmth. I got up. I went to the window for a breath of air. I tell you I drank it in."

"The morning air is sweet," said Fabrizze.

"Have a care," said Mendone. "There's a chill in it."

"I was thirsty," said Bassetti. "I took a glass of water."

"Clear and cold," said Fabrizze.

"Almost as good as wine," said Mendone.

"I had an orange," said Bassetti. "And bread and coffee."

"The food was delicious," said Fabrizze.

"I went out for a walk," said Bassetti. "The trees were fresh in the wind. Birds were singing. The warmth of the sun reached into my bones. I saw a smile here and there

81

among the neighbors. Children were playing. And then I heard music. It was Igino playing the harmonica. They say it's a song of love."

"Beauty on every side," said Fabrizze.

"And trouble enough into the bargain," said Mendone.

"I came here," said Bassetti. "It was enough to make an old man suspicious. And so I came looking for Mendone."

"I was sleeping," said Mendone. "I was trying to recover from the day before."

"I used to ask for things," said Bassetti. "I asked for this and that and the other. And now? Now I ask for life."

The kitchen was fragrant with pipe smoke. His rich soothing voice filled the house.

"There it is," said Fabrizze.

The gentle hands were sending hope and love into every corner of his being.

V

A CHILD was born after the turn of the year. He had blue eyes and a circle of reddish gold hair. They called him Paul. Fabrizze remarked that he came before his time with a smile.

"Why wouldn't he smile?" said Grace. "He saw red wine in every corner of the house. It was under the beds and in the closets. It was in pints and quarts and gallons. It was in five-gallon jugs and barrels. The glow of it was in the eyes of his father and his great-grandfather. Their lips were as dark as cherries with it. And the house was filled with laughing strangers."

Fabrizze and Mendone started to make wine in the fall.

They put up three barrels of juice for fermenting and then realized that everyone was doing the same with the same blue grapes. They emptied the juice into jugs and cleaned the barrels to be sure there was no sour stinging taste in the wine. They began to experiment. Mendone bought a basket of the muscatel grapes. He pressed and boiled them. He skimmed them and poured the juice into one of the barrels.

"It helps to clear the Concord wine," he said. "And it gives that bit of sweetness. Wait until you taste it."

"Buy more of the red grapes," said Fabrizze. "We'll try the ones called Catawba and Delaware."

"We'll keep mixing," said Mendone.

"A gallon here, a gallon there," said Fabrizze.

"We'll keep tasting," said Mendone.

"We'll swim in this wine," said Fabrizze.

"I hear it's good to cut in a few apples," said Mendone.

Mendone discovered other good things. It was good to make wine by the light of candles. It was good to sip wine while making wine. A bit of music was good with wine. It was very good to lift your glass to the soft light and hear a mother singing sweet persuasion to a child unborn. Finally, it was good to be with a younger man who would put the candles out and help you up the stairs when work was finished in the wintry night.

All their wine was sold before the holidays. Men came across the city for it. They promised to bring friends and so Mendone put in an order to buy twelve barrels of juice from a cumpare of Penza.

"It isn't right," sad Grace. "It isn't right."

84

"What's this?" said Mendone. "I don't understand."

"It's getting away from you," said Grace.

"Never, never," said Mendone. "This wine will be even better."

"Drink to it," said Fabrizze.

"First you bought the grapes," said Grace. "You cleaned them and pressed the juice. Now you buy the juice. After this you'll be buying the wine itself. You'll have to look the other way when you sell it. But then you'll have someone to sell it for you."

"Wonderful," said Mendone. "Drink to it."

"She runs us through," said Fabrizze.

"And it isn't right to take money in the house," said Grace.

"This will be the last of it," said Fabrizze. "Still, I like to have people around me. It's nothing more than that, Grace, and no one believes it. A man was telling me about his brother. 'Bring him here,' I said. 'I'd like to see him.' He thought it was to sell wine. I just wanted to see his brother. Listen then. I've been thinking of a place of my own. A store perhaps."

"Find a store then," said Grace.

"I talked to Rossi about it," said Fabrizze. "He'll put money in with me. All we do on the job is take walks and see that the switches are clean. The other day we sharpened the tools and put them aside. The only excitement is what's in the lunches."

The experiments with wine continued. Jugs were hidden everywhere. Fabrizze and Mendone filled strange black bottles with a blend so imaginative that neither of them could remember the ingredients. They boiled the corks and drove them in and buried the black bottles under the basement floor. They drank a toast from the first barrel. Something was lacking in there. They went on tasting and mixing. Deep into the night Grace heard the bubbling and pouring and whispering.

"Must you lose sleep with this wine?" she said.

"Wine, wine," said Mendone, frying sausage in it.

"Wine warms you in the winter," said Fabrizze. "Wine cools you in the summer."

"Wine helps the digestion," said Mendone. "Wine enriches the blood. Wine is good for the skin."

"Wine puts a certain light in the eyes," said Fabrizze.

"Is it good for the lungs?" said Grace. "The baby cries out when I take him in the fresh air."

"Wine keeps the teeth clean," said Mendone.

"And it loosens the tongue," said Grace.

"But then it relieves the heart," said Fabrizze.

"And fills our pockets," said Mendone.

Profits were mounting. Fabrizze made more money in the basement than on the railroad. Along with it came a fair share of disruption in the house. Part of the railroad gang followed Fabrizze home in the afternoon to take a glass with him. They lingered in the cool basement. Now and again they asked Fabrizze to read from the daily paper. They sipped wine and made comments on the news.

"There's a shock," Cardino would say.

"Listen for another," said Rumbone.

Fabrizze went on reading.

"There it is," said Gritti.

86

"Enough of that," said Cardino. "Turn the page."

"Here is news," said Fabrizze. "It's time for supper."

"One more glass," said Gritti.

"Your wife is waiting," said Fabrizze.

"There's a shock," said Rumbone.

Day and night there were customers in the house. The tailor Salupo planted himself in the corner and waited for customers of his own. A measuring tape was round his neck. Rainbow garters choked his sleeves. He kept giving the garters to children. He winked and beckoned when he saw a child. Suddenly he was whispering of a secret thing. He whispered until the child was cross-eyed with wonder and delight.

"Sit on my knee," Salupo would say, softly. "I was watching for you. I was watching and waiting and when I saw you I said to myself, 'Look, look, look: here's the little boy with brown hair: tell him the secret!' Listen, listen, listen. Put your ear closer and closer. Have you heard about the box hidden up in my attic? Listen then. Up in the corner of the closet in the attic is a box, a big box, a big red box, a box bigger than a little boy with brown hair just like you. And the box is full, the big box is loaded up, the big red box is spilling over with toys, toys, toys. Look with me in the box, the big box, the big red box. Look, look. Bouncing balls and yellow balloons. Red wagons and spinning tops. Puppies and clowns and horns to blow. A long black train with smoke and a whistle. Silver bells and a boat with a sail. A can of paint and a bottle of glue. Are you listening? Tell your mother to bring you to the closet in the attic. I'll be waiting there with the big red box. Look again. A rocking horse and a big bass drum. Hammers and nails and wooden spoons. Chocolate cookies and rubber bands. Pails and wheels and marching soldiers. Come closer. I'll give you this garter from my sleeve. Think of me in the closet of the attic with the big red box of toys, toys, toys. I'll be waiting for you. It's a secret thing. Shake hands on it."

Often Salupo came upstairs to talk with Grace and play with the baby. He would thread imaginary needles and measure Paul for a suit and sew it up on the spot.

"How he watches me," he said. "Look at that smile. I wish I could sew his trouble in a sack and drop the sack in the sea."

"As long as he has no more than his share," said Grace.

"Next year I'll make a suit for him," said Salupo. "Blue as his eyes. Running through it will be a stitch of gold to match his hair. And let me design a dress for you. I have this brown cloth. Perfect, perfect. And why doesn't Fabrizze come to me? I can do a remarkable thing for him."

The lovely look of Grace and the child sent Salupo back downstairs for more wine. He drank and drank and brooded over the fact that he had never married. He staggered round the basement insulting everyone. He put his hand on Gritti.

"You make your own clothes, eh?" he said.

He caught Cardino by the coat.

"Who goes here?" he said.

He reeled outside and up to his attic in the red rooming house. He leaned out the window and called down to passing women.

"You there," he said. "You with the black hair!"

"I beg your pardon?"

"I'll make a dress for you!" said Salupo. "Among other things! Come up here for a fitting! Just the two of us! Come up, come up! Eight flights to love! Who's the old man? You there! Move away from that girl!"

"Move away? I'm her husband! I'll come up there and teach you a lesson! Animal, animal!"

"Animal is right!" said Salupo. "Like a lion! Come up, come up! I dare you! Eight flights to death! Wait, wait! Don't move! I'm coming to you!"

Up the stairs rushed the husband.

Salupo locked himself in the closet. He sat on his high stool and puffed a cigar. He tried to sell a suit.

"I was teasing," he said, behind the door. "It's a way to get the customers in. I went too far with it, eh? Risky, risky. Last week I was beaten something terrible. The truth is, I have a cloth for you. On the second rack there. An imported silk. The black, the black. You deserve the best. What a defender of the family! How proud your wife must be! Tell me her name."

"She carries my name."

"She should carry it like a flag," said Salupo.

"What happened to the lion?"

"What a sense of humor," said Salupo. "But you're upset, eh? Come and see me tomorrow. Bring the children. I have a big box in here. A big red box."

"Now I know you. Never mind with that big red box. My nephew couldn't sleep thinking of it."

Another caller at the house on Jackson Street was Tony

Cucuzza. Tony played the guitar for his friends and he gambled at cards for a living. He was half blind in the left eye and he kept the right one closed unless he saw a woman, or a chance to double his money.

"How is it going?" someone would say.

"I'm winning," said Tony. "Yesterday I won. The day before I won. Today I won. I win and win and win. But then one day the game is over. And that's all."

Tony would play his guitar on the porch and Grace would hurry out the back door. Tony tricked her. He would strum on the step and then run to catch her leaving by the back. One day he started playing in front and he waited right there. A moment later Grace came headlong into his arms.

"I win again," said Tony. He ripped off his cap and his coil of black hair jumped up. "You think I'm from the woods, eh? Look here. I brought something for Paul. A deck of cards. He'll sort them out."

"It's thoughtful of you," said Grace.

"They spread these rumors about me," said Tony. "They say I'm a gambler and I make trouble. Isn't that what they tell you?"

"I've heard it," said Grace.

"Who tells you?" said Tony. "Who says it?"

Grace looked away.

"Never mind then," said Tony. "You have nothing to fear from me. I respect you and your husband. . . . It's time for the walk."

Tony appointed himself watchdog. Strumming his guitar he followed Grace and the baby down the street. His right eye closed in exultance and his dark wild head was dancing time to the melody.

A stranger happened to turn and speak to Grace. She blushed and moved on. Tony spun his cap to screw it down tighter. Smiling, he walked over to the man.

"Hold still," said Tony, with his set smile. Two front teeth were missing and it seemed his laughter would come pouring through to darken the day. "Hold still," he was saying. "I may take your picture. Something to remember you. Look behind me. Tony Cucuzza throws a long shadow, eh? You know what I mean?"

Tony began to squeeze his arm. Presently they were both up on tiptoe. Tony was smiling.

"Give me your hand," he whispered. "I want you to feel how my heart is pounding. You know what I mean?"

"I know, I know," said the victim.

It was Tony Cucuzza who provided music for that first party in the house on Jackson Street. He was caught in the midst of preparations for it. He helped to decorate the basement. He carried invitations like threats through the neighborhood. One afternoon he sang the baby to sleep while Grace was making fresh sausage.

"They spread these rumors," said Fabrizze. "They say you sang a lullaby and took a nap with Paul. I knew it was in you."

"It's you and your wife," said Tony. "You put things in me and then you find them."

"You'll be here to play for us on Saturday?"

"But what is this party?" said Tony. "Tell me the reason for it. I hear different things from everyone."

91

"Choose a reason," said Fabrizze. "Soon I'll be a citizen of this country. One thing more. A girl is coming from Italy. She's called Lucia and she's coming to marry Mancini. One thing more. I made the last payment on the house. One thing more. I have a location for a store. I'll know for sure in a day or two."

"And nothing more?" said Tony.

"It's April," said Fabrizze. "We'll be together."

And so they were.

The basement was packed with friends. Tony played a song of welcome for the lovely Lucia. Afterwards he sat beside the stairs to salute each of the guests as they arrived. He played songs of welcome until he coaxed from the night a complete stranger.

First came Lucia.

"Look, Fabrizze, look," said Mancini, flushed with wine. "Is she what we thought? Here's the picture."

"Put the picture away," said Fabrizze. "The girl is here and you look at the picture. What a beauty she is. I see the blue of her eyes across the room. Such color in her cheek."

"I can't believe it," said Mancini. "I can't believe it."

"But why are you so shy?" said Fabrizze. "She's waiting there for you. Ask her to dance."

"She says nothing," said Mancini, helplessly. "She blushes if I go near. She's disappointed in me. I feel it."

"What more can she say?" said Fabrizze. "She came thousands of miles for you. Wait then. Rumbone is asking her to dance. Look out for him. A dangerous one."

Mancini went after more wine.

Adelina swept Fabrizze into the dance.

"Talk to me a little," said the old lady.

"They say your husband was a fine dancer," said Fabrizze.

"It was all dancing and talking," said Adelina. "Sweet words, Fabrizze, and not a bone in him. Not a bone. I knew it before I married him. I foresaw it!"

"And you took him in spite of it," said Fabrizze, proud of her.

"What is it?"

"I say you took him in spite of it!" said Fabrizze, immensely proud of her.

"That was the reason!" said Adelina, bursting into laughter.

Mancini was pulling Fabrizze by the arm.

"Come aside," said Mancini. "The dance is over. Rumbone is gone. There she is again. All by herself."

"It's a good chance for you," said Fabrizze. "Are you ready? But she knows we're talking about her. How alert! How she blushes! She's turning away. Look at her ear!"

"Her ear? Which one?"

"Control yourself," said Fabrizze. "Look, look. Her ear is like a pearl. Are you ready? Wait, wait. Poggio is asking her to dance. A dangerous one."

"A curse on him," said Mancini, softly.

Josephine was celebrating at the table. She closed her eyes and popped a cherry pepper into her mouth. She sat there in horror as it blazed through her.

"These hot peppers will finish me," she said.

She speared a link of sausage.

"Too much pork is bad," she said.

She loaded her dish with endive. She flirted with codfish in a salad of garlic and parsley and olive oil.

"Why so much garlic?" she said.

She tasted the fish and found it good. She drained her wine and filled the glass. She closed her eyes and popped a pepper into her mouth. A sudden bewildered look was on her face.

"It's time for the sausage again," said Mendone.

"You mock an old lady," said Josephine. "Remember, Mendone, I have only two teeth left."

"One for meat and one for bread," said Mendone. "Let's see if there's a dance left inside you."

Mancini drew Fabrizze behind the barrels.

"Where were you?" said Mancini. "Where did you go?"

"But why are you following me?" said Fabrizze.

"She's alone."

"Ask her to dance."

"Help me, Fabrizze, help me."

"Get hold of yourself."

"I don't know what's happening," said Mancini. "I was going over to her. I forgot her name! I couldn't think of it. I was looking around for you. My knees were all water. She was watching me. She was waiting. What's happening to me? Tell me what to do! I'm depending on you!"

"Come with me," said Fabrizze. "Put the glass down. Put the picture away. Tony will play a tarantella. We'll get you together in the dance. Squeeze her hand and say nothing."

The dance lasted half an hour. Tony played the same

stirring melody over and over. The dancers closed into a circle. They followed the music. They followed so close that it turned into a chase. There were two and three and four steps to the beat. Tony lost control of it. Suddenly he threw the guitar aside and jumped in with the dancers. They formed a circle round Lucia and Mancini. They whirled and clapped and stamped the floor. Wild cries went up. It seemed they would bring down the house.

"Faster, faster!"

"Round and round!"

"Wake up there!"

"Back in line!"

"Show me something!"

"Once more!"

"And again!"

"Out with it!"

"Faster, faster!"

"I'm dizzy!"

"Let me out!"

It was a cry for mercy that ended it.

They sat round four tables to eat and drink. Fabrizze went upstairs. He returned with an old blackened bulb of provolone cheese. He set it before Rumbone who got up and moved away.

"Look here," said Fabrizze. "Look at this."

"It reminds me of Gritti before he shaves," said Rumbone.

"Everything reminds you of Gritti," said Gritti.

"I bought this cheese the other day," said Fabrizze. "I went to an import house on the East Side."

"And they told you it was a cheese," said Rumbone.

"It came from Italy," said Fabrizze.

"Try to understand," said Rumbone. "They got rid of it. And now you have it. Get rid of it."

"The black look means nothing," said Fabrizze. "Do you see the red seal? A man called Amaro says he'll stand or fall by this bulb of cheese. He left his name and address."

"It's like a slap in the face," said Rumbone.

"I'll cut it," said Fabrizze. "Where is Cardino? Come closer, Cardino, come closer. Bend down. I go in with the knife. How rich and creamy! Look at Cardino! He felt something when it opened!"

"But I did," said Cardino, startled.

"I choose you to taste and judge it," said Fabrizze. "First a glass of wine to rinse your mouth. You were puffing on that cigar. Wait, wait. You must forget everything but this cheese. Cheese, Cardino, cheese. Study it there."

"It's like butter," said Cardino.

"Are you ready?" said Fabrizze. "Don't bite it. Let a piece of it rest on your tongue. Here is a kiss from Amaro!"

Cardino was upset even before he put the cheese on his tongue. He sat there leaning forward in the chair. His eyes held Fabrizze. Suddenly his mouth fell open. It seemed he would fall on his face.

"The cheese is gone!" he said.

"It's like a smoke!" said Fabrizze.

"I feel it everywhere!"

"It's going through you!" said Fabrizze.

"Needles of it!"

"It's like music!" said Fabrizze. "There's no end to it!"

"This cursed cheese is alive!" cried Cardino.

"Everyone taste it," said Fabrizze. "Let it melt. Wine for everyone. Back to the cheese. To the wine. To the cheese. A bit of music with it!"

"Sharp and strong!"

"It seizes me!"

"Put it away then!"

They finished it on the spot.

"I know the surprise," said Rumbone. "You sent for Amaro."

"Listen then," said Fabrizze. "I went to this import house to buy cheese and ham for the people who drink wine here. And for the party tonight. I passed the market on the way home. There was an empty store across the street. I've been thinking of a store. Why not an Italian store right there?"

"Why not?" said Penza. "How easy it is. Did you hear him? He had an idea. Benedico! I haven't had an idea in ten years. Do it, Fabrizze, do it. It's a good idea."

"It's done," said Grace.

"Let me go over this," said Penza. "First he had an idea and then he went ahead with it. This is very good."

"Rossi and I leased the store," said Fabrizze. "He'll stay on the railroad and I'll manage it. Mancini will fix the inside. It should be ready toward the end of summer. And I wrote a letter to Amaro. I told him I want the best of everything."

"A toast to the store," said Bassetti.

"Wait, wait," said Fabrizze. "Another surprise."

Poggio was digging in the corner of the basement.

"It was Cardino who taught me this," said Fabrizze. "Deeper, Poggio, deeper. What a worker! Find a treasure there and you go back on the railroad! Gently now."

Poggio unearthed four gleaming black bottles of wine.

"Here is wine for the toast," said Fabrizze. "Wait till you taste it. Glasses for everyone!"

"Never mind," said Cardino. "Pass the bottles!"

"Many lovely things to you!" said Fabrizze.

"My blood is boiling with this wine!"

"It's in my bones!"

"I'm done for!"

"I have to rest a little," said Poggio.

There was a dance to end the party.

Grace and Fabrizze walked the old people home.

"Take my arm," said Josephine, to her sister.

"I'm holding Bassetti," said Adelina.

"Take hold of someone sure to stand," said Bassetti. "I'll hold Grace."

They strolled down the warm fragrant night. One by one they slipped away. Igino was playing the harmonica in some high hidden corner. Tony challenged him on the guitar. They came together in a song. Laughter filled the street and soared in the night to set the stars dancing.

Fabrizze was helping Bassetti up the stairs.

"Be careful," said Fabrizze.

"I have no choice," said Bassetti. "A fine party. We'll see what tomorrow brings."

"Let it bring you to the house for supper," said Fabrizze.

He and Grace were hand in hand following Mendone

home. They could still hear Tony playing and singing to himself in the night. A soft loving wind left the leaves all sighing with its presence and its loss. Mendone puffed his pipe. He was thinking of his career in the store.

"From this moment I'm a man of business," he said, over his shoulder. "I smile only on the holidays. . . . Now who is this?"

A man was rapping their door.

He wore a derby and his feet were tapping to the distant music of the guitar.

"Good evening," said Mendone. "You've come for a room?"

The stranger turned his dark merry eyes on Mendone.

"Who are you?" said Mendone.

"I heard the music," said the stranger, in Italian.

His voice had a rich lilting quality.

Seeing Grace he bowed and swept off his derby as though he had caught a fallen star just for her. His feet were tapping and yet suddenly there was no music anywhere.

"I am Vivolo," he said.

VI

THE store was an immediate success.

It was located within a block of the teeming outdoor central market. Shoppers for fruit and vegetables would pass by and then come back to see what Fabrizze had to offer. They were held by the fragrance of cheese and salami and olives. Lingering, they peered into the cool dark interior of the store. Cheese was hanging from the rafters in bulbs of soft gold light. Among them were hard rods of salami and great bulging hams. The hams had been rolled in red or black pepper and packed as though for all time. There were red rings of devil pepper and slabs of cured lard. Suddenly there was the strange mingled

100

sweetness of basil and thyme and origan. It seemed that the door had swung open here to reveal the chamber where spicy food was stored.

"You arrive just in time," said Mendone.

"Then you speak Italian?"

"Speak it?" said Mendone. "I sing it and write it, too. Come in, my friend, come in."

"Whose picture is in the window?"

"The greatest singer in the world," said Mendone. "A voice so strong it blows your hat off."

"Such a little smile he has."

"Do you see a smile?" said Mendone.

"Isn't he smiling?"

"Some say yes and some say no," said Mendone.

"Now he isn't smiling. But who is he?"

The fact is, Fabrizze had set in the window an oval picture of Augustine taken in youth. Augustine sat there holding his knees as though the chair was getting hot. He had a flag of black hair and a rampant moustache. His head was cocked in the way of one listening for the fatal footfall.

"I have a feeling I know this face," said Rossi, on his first visit before the opening. "What a strange look. He's leaning and listening. Something worries him."

"You may be right," said Fabrizze. "His wife just gave birth to a second son."

"Who is he?" said Rossi. "Why is his picture here?"

"For inspiration," said Fabrizze. "He's the famous mountain climber of the north. A man with fire at his heels. They say he outruns most things. And the rest he outclimbs."

"They'll say it as long as he does it," said Rossi. "And then they won't say it."

"Come and see the store."

"It's that smile I remember from somewhere," said Rossi. "Now you see it and now you don't. The man is tricky, eh? But I know this face! Tell me, tell me!"

"After you see the store," said Fabrizze. "Come this way. I want you to study the arrangement. Here are open barrels of olives. Green and black and brown. The customer steals an olive and we take him prisoner. Help yourself. Look up. Ham and cheese and salami swing from the ceiling. Come along. Pick your way past the crates and sacks. Everything is torn open. Dried codfish and horse beans. Mushrooms and chestnuts. Wild onions and sleeping snails."

"Sleeping snails?"

"They wake up in the water," said Fabrizze. "We used to wait for them near the stone walls. They come out when it rains. Look there. Lentils and coffee. Nuts and figs and Saint John's bread."

"Saint John's bread? It's like old sticks."

"The saint was lost in the forest," said Fabrizze. "He lived for weeks on these alone."

"Why should a saint be lost in the forest?"

"It's what they say," said Fabrizze. "Perhaps they mean the forest as the world. Look here then. Open these jars. Basil and thyme and fennel. Origan and hot pepper."

"Why is your hand in my pocket?" said Rossi.

"No customer escapes."

"Stop, stop," said Rossi. "You go too far."

102

"I'm sprinkling origan in your coat," said Fabrizze. "Nancy will fall into your arms when you go home. Look here. All kinds of spaghetti. Shells and pipes. Elbows and butterflies. Here is pastine like stars. Let me put stars in your soup. And now the tour is over. On the floor to your left is an empty crate. Pick it up. Fill it before you leave. Buy, Rossi, buy. The profit is half yours."

"Profit?" said Rossi. "I'll be satisfied to break even with the men you picked to work here. Mancini is all right. At least he's a married man. He'll think twice."

"What's wrong with Rumbone?"

"I'll tell you about Rumbone," said Rossi. "He quit the railroad last week. Only three men remember him doing any work there. Would you believe it? Three men. And one of them isn't too sure. This Rumbone is like a ghost."

"And Poggio?"

"He refuses to work. Ask him. He'll tell you in your face. I found him in the tool shed the other morning. He was fanning himself. He was fanning himself at eight o'clock in the morning."

"And Bassetti?"

"Too old to work. And who's this behind the counter?"

"A special assistant. His name is Mendone."

"He watches me like a hawk," said Rossi.

"It's because you buy nothing. Come closer. It took seventy years to bring us this face. How the eyes are quick and alert!"

"Fear," said Mendone.

"How fresh his color," said Fabrizze. "He's aglow."

"Wine," said Mendone.

103

"Here is peace," said Fabrizze.

"I'm tired," said Mendone.

"Where are the white gloves?" said Rossi. "Put them on and cut me half a Genoa salami. I want a fresh one cut."

"And you want the better half," said Mendone.

Rossi took Fabrizze aside.

"McGuire sent word," said Rossi. "There'll be a place for you as long as he's with the railroad. Do you know what happened the other day? I went with him on an inspection. We were riding the track smoothly. 'A bed put in by Fabrizze,' I told him. And then the engine was pounding and shaking. 'A stretch by Gallagher,' I said. 'At least it keeps the engineer awake,' he said. We were going smooth again. 'This is Fabrizze?' he said. 'So it is,' I said. 'Fabrizze had a way of tamping ties,' I said, 'and no one seems to know the secret.' And then the train was jumping. 'I'll tell you the secret,' he said. 'The secret is intelligence.' "

"Bring him to the grand opening," said Fabrizze. "We'll fill a basket for him. Saturday is the day. Our location is perfect. Hundreds of shoppers come to the market. Trolley cars stop across the street. It's even within walking distance of the main square. There'll be music here. This table will be spread with food. I want people to taste before buying. They'll strip us from floor to ceiling. We'll make a fortune."

"And then?"

"We'll spend it," said Fabrizze.

He guessed right about the opening.

All day the store was packed. Igino stayed outside and played the harmonica under a rainbow of balloons tied to his shoulder. It seemed he had dropped in from a land of song and play. Inside Tony strummed the guitar to set a furious pace. Bassetti and Mancini were trapped behind the counter. Rumbone carried olives and candy to people waiting at the trolley stop. Poggio kept soaring up the ladder out of the crowd to pluck down cheese and ham from the ceiling. Once he was sent up for provolone.

"How's this one?" he said.

"No, no, no," said the customer. "I don't want it!"

"They're all the same," said Poggio.

"Don't tell me about it!" shouted the customer.

"A little louder," said Poggio. "I can't hear you."

"I want the one in the corner! The one out of the light! That one or nothing!"

For a moment the crowd was breathless as Poggio held a salami and reached far into the corner. Gasping, he called for a knife.

"Why doesn't he come down and move the ladder?" said a voice.

"Be quiet," said another.

"Where are you?" said Poggio, straining. "Let me hear your voice again. Is this the cheese you want?"

"That's the one!"

"Come over here," said Poggio. "One more step. One more step. Stand still. Hold your hands out."

Poggio slashed the string and the provolone fell on the man's head. He buckled there.

"Is that the one?" said Poggio.

"I'm not so sure," said the customer, rubbing his head.

"How about a ham?" said Poggio.

"You'll finish me on the spot, eh?"

A man called Ravello was charmed off the trolley by the song of the harmonica. He came over to investigate. He peered through the door. People swept him in from behind. He was trapped there in the crowd. Fabrizze appeared six inches away with a smile so engaging and eyes so clear that Ravello smiled back with all his heart. He felt like a child. Fabrizze put cheese and bread in his left hand while pinching his arm in sudden affection. Fabrizze was swallowed by the crowd. Ravello went after him. An elbow was driven into his neck. His hat was knocked off. He retrieved it and here was Fabrizze with flaming hair and deep soft eyes and that nose like a command. Ravello was longing to be pinched. Fabrizze put salami on his bread and vanished. Someone filled his right hand with wet olives. He wound up in the corner with Tony Cucuzza who whispered and smiled in a way that sent him back into the crowd.

"You there," he said. "Are you Rumbone? The man with the guitar says you'll take care of me. I want a quarter of a pound of Romano cheese. And that's all."

"A quarter of a pound?" said Rumbone. "You have mice?"

"Where are you going?" said Ravello.

"Come with me," said Rumbone.

Rumbone led him back to the storeroom and gave him a glass of wine. They drank several toasts and then came

106

out. Rumbone caught sight of a girl filling the doorway with light and beauty.

"Mendone," he said. "Take care of Ravello here. He's waiting an hour for a quarter pound of Romano."

"Not a quarter of a pound," said Mendone.

"Are you a clerk?" said Ravello, following him.

Mendone poured wine in the storeroom. He was wearing a white apron. A yellow pencil was behind his ear.

"It's a good thing I came into your hands," said Ravello.

"Have another glass then," said Mendone.

"I saw this face in the crowd," said Ravello. "I was feeling reckless out there."

Fabrizze slipped in for a glass of wine.

"Look who's here," he said.

"I saw you out there," said Ravello.

"I remember you," said Fabrizze, pinching him. "Did you taste the figs from Sicily?"

"Where are the figs?" said Ravello, helplessly.

"Look for me before you leave," said Fabrizze. "Let me thank you for stopping in. I'll have something for you."

"What is it?" said Ravello.

"A surprise," said Fabrizze.

"Really? Will you show me the figs?"

Rumbone had pounced on the girl.

"I want some olives," she said.

"How easy to please," said Rumbone, bowing and smiling. "This way, my dear. Make room there. Now which do you prefer? Black or brown or green. Let's taste them."

Rumbone plunged into a barrel and came up with a

shining black olive. He held it like a pearl and then insisted on popping it into her mouth.

"A pound of the black?" he said. "You make up your mind in a flash! And what else? Say the word. Come closer."

The girl blushed and turned away.

"But I think I know," said Rumbone. "You'd like to taste the other olives, eh? You're ashamed to say it. How sweet."

Twice more he popped olives into her mouth.

"And what else?" he said. "Come closer. I can't hear a thing with this crowd. Such beautiful eyes. What an idea I have! It's for a summer afternoon, my dear. A barrel of olives and a bit of wine. And you. And nothing more."

"I want bay leaf, if you please."

"So polite," said Rumbone. "And she wants bay leaf. But what will you do with bay leaf?"

"We put it in spaghetti sauce," said the girl, softly.

"It sweetens the sauce, eh? How she takes hold of things. And what else? Come closer, my dear. This crowd, this crowd."

"Fennel?" said the girl, afraid to risk it.

"Fennel, fennel," said Rumbone, delighted. "But what are your plans with this fennel?"

"My father makes sausage."

"He makes sausage!" cried Rumbone. "Benedico! As though he hadn't done enough!"

Ravello was being served. His voice boomed through the store.

"Cheese, cheese," he said, pounding the counter. "Give me a pound of Romano then! How much is that piece?"

"Over a pound," said Mendone.

"Over a pound?"

"Almost two pounds," said Mendone.

"Almost two."

"Exactly two and one quarter," said Mendone. "It's just right for you. The other piece is too much. It's almost three pounds."

"But it may be five after all," said Ravello. "Make an end of this. Give me the small one."

Carrying two great bags Ravello struggled out to the sidewalk. Rumbone was telling the girl about Augustine.

"A famous watchman," said Rumbone. "We must watch for love, he says, and take it where we find it. How he watches us!"

Ravello set his bags down and mopped his brow.

"Here is Ravello," said Rumbone. "Did you get the balloons for your children?"

"Balloons?" said Ravello.

"Let me light your cigar," said Rumbone.

"It never ends," said Ravello, half to himself. "I had music. I had wine. I was leaving when the man with the golden hair gave me a box of torrone candy. We went back and took a few glasses to my health. He put a cigar in my mouth. He invited me to his house for supper. Now it's balloons. Give me the red and the blue then. And put me back on the trolley. I started out to buy a hat."

Late in the afternoon Vivolo came tapping with his cane. He wore a black suit and his black derby. The derby was like a cork forcing power down through his dark brilliant eyes. There was a dash of gray at his temples. He glanced at Fabrizze and smiled, as if to say, "Come, come, Fabrizze: what tricks are you playing on these people here?"

Fabrizze went round the counter. He heard Vivolo speaking in rich precise Italian.

"My dear lady, my dear lady," said Vivolo.

"What is it, what is it?"

"You're standing on my foot," said Vivolo.

"I'm sorry!"

"Now it's the other foot," said Vivolo, confiding.

"I'm sorry, I'm sorry! A strange dialect you speak."

"Yours is even stranger," said Vivolo.

"Vivolo," said Fabrizze. "Can I help you?"

"Some citrate," said Vivolo. "The Brioschi. And I'd like some cheese. Let me taste what you have there."

Fabrizze cut a slice of provolone and passed it over. A man intercepted it and swallowed it, neatly.

"Good appetite," said Vivolo. "Some bread?"

Fabrizze passed another slice.

"Too sharp and strong," said Vivolo. "I want something mild. Something to alert me."

He bought a bulb of mozzarella cheese. Fabrizze walked him to the door and asked his opinion of the business.

"You'll do well," said Vivolo. "I was watching Mendone. The people gather around him. They'll wait and wait for him. It's good the way he handles the food."

Suddenly Vivolo was dancing aside. He swept off his derby as Grace guided Paul in his stroller through the door.

"Good afternoon," she said, smiling.

110

"I'm comical?" said Vivolo.

"Forgive me," said Grace.

"A pleasure," said Vivolo.

"It's your derby," said Grace. "I have the feeling that something will jump out when you do that."

Something did jump out. A man with an armful of bags blundered against Vivolo and a jar of peppers jumped out. Vivolo caught it before it hit the floor. So quick was his movement that no one could follow it. He replaced the jar and turned to Grace and Fabrizze. His gold pivot tooth flashed in a smile.

"Good luck with the store," he said. "And good day to you."

He bowed out.

"Did you see that?" said Grace.

"Rumbone says he's a panther," said Fabrizze.

"I was still watching the jar," said Grace. "And he had it!"

"An exciting man."

"I wonder where he goes in the day," said Grace.

Mendone came round the counter.

"I'll take the child for a breath of air," he said. "We'll be closing the store in a while."

"Go for a walk, Paul," said Grace. "But why are you looking like that? What's to be done with such a boy?"

Mendone invited him to shake hands.

"What a fellow you are," said Mendone. "We kiss every morning and still I have to introduce myself in the afternoons. Come along through the market. We'll see our friends again."

Paul offered his hand and looked away.

"Look, look," said Mendone. "Your hand fits in mine. But we belong to each other, eh?"

He pushed the stroller outside.

The two rows of market stands were divided by a walk. Late sun slanted beneath the roof as though drawn here for a long look at this feast of color. Owners of stands were lounging and talking in the soft light. They were ready to close down for the weekend. Each one seemed to be waiting for his neighbor to make the move.

The potato seller called out when she saw Mendone.

"It's Mendone," she said. "He has time for old friends."

"Not Mendone?" said the owner of the next stand.

"It is Mendone," said the next.

Suddenly the name was being carried all the way down the aisle. It reached the far stand where Piconi stood smiling over his watermelons. Piconi leaned forward.

"Is it Paul?" he said, shading his eyes.

"Paul is there."

"Come here, Paul, come here."

"Watermelon, Paul, watermelon."

"Peaches, Paul, peaches."

"Plums for Paul."

And now the boy's name was round and about like a summons to delight from every side.

"Where is this Paul?"

"Paul is there."

"Show me this Paul."

Paul took hold of the bar of the stroller. He rose up as if to make a speech. His eyes opened wide as he heard his

112

name filling the day. He was so thrilled that he lost balance and tumbled backward into his seat. Laughter was everywhere.

"So this is Paul," said Sisto. "I keep secrets. Tell me what Paul will be when he grows up."

"Tell him," said Mendone. "Tell Sisto you'll be a man."

Paul gurgled with a strange sure emphasis at the end.

"Did he say it?" said Sisto, startled.

"Did you hear it?" said Mendone.

"I thought I did," said Sisto.

"But then he said it," said Mendone.

"And not even a year he has," said Sisto. "Why, it's enough to be a man. A peach as gold as your hair for such a response."

"And for the teacher?" said Mendone.

"A peach for the teacher," said Sisto.

Barbieri was leaning over his mound of blue plums. He sniffed the air. He blinked in amazement and looked again.

"Look at this," he said. "Is it wheels under Paul? But he's on the move before he walks."

"We must make room for the young," said Mendone.

"This America, this America," said Barbieri.

Old man and boy made their way up one side of the market and came down the other side. The boy was fascinated by the colors and shapes. They changed and changed again. His mouth fell open at the swollen green watermelons. All at once there was a full red smiling cut, and the sweetness of it melted away inside him. Here and there Mendone stopped to talk with friends.

"What's this pencil on your ear?" said Teresa. "You've

come a long way since cleaning my celery, eh? Can you write something?"

"It isn't necessary," said Mendone.

"How the child gazes at me," said Teresa. "No one has looked that long in thirty years! What is it he sees, madonna mia, what is it he sees? Let me clean a carrot for him. I'm a woman of business, Mendone, and so I trade him a carrot for a kiss."

Mendone started away.

"Wait then," said Teresa.

"What is it?"

"Take something," said Teresa. "Wait, wait. Here is a fine red pepper for you. Roast it on the stove. I had it set aside. I was going to take it home."

"Save it then," said Mendone.

"I want you to have it," said Teresa. "I just remembered it. I remembered it for you."

Mendone and Paul reached the last of the stands.

"Are you leaving then?"

"Come again, Paul, come again."

"Goodbye, Mendone."

Their names were carried down the cool sweet aisle to Piconi who stood there in the last glow of sunlight. Piconi twirled his moustache in triumph and threw a kiss. Mendone lifted Paul to his shoulder. He was teaching the child to throw a kiss.

"Leave a kiss for your friends," he said.

Paul hid his face.

"Look, Paul, look," said Sisto.

Paul peeked out.

114

"A kiss for Paul!"
Laughter was heard.
"Come again, Paul."
"Goodbye, Mendone, goodbye."
"Mendone—Mendone."

VII

DEATH came to Mendone in the night.
He was set forth in the house on Jackson Street. Three
days and three nights the candles were burning beside the
great coffin. There was the slow black march of the mourn-
ers. Hour after hour the anguished cries went up. Grief
and sorrow flooded into every corner of the old house.
Toward the end it seemed to Grace that death was the
wild blind king of the world.

By the third day everyone had told a tale.

"Mendone worked for me in the market," said Teresa.
"When he started I never used to show the prices of
things. I'd change the prices for different people. Some of

the customers never ask you the price. It's the gentle ones. They're ashamed. You can see it. I'd raise the price three or four cents. And then I'd turn around. Mendone would be watching me. Not a word from him. But something was in his mouth. It was dragging that moustache down. And then one morning I was looking in the mirror. All at once I looked just like he did. From then on I showed the prices."

"I'll tell you how it was with my husband," said a woman. "He finished shaving. He was teasing me. He said the funeral director wouldn't have to shave him. He died on the spot! Right there at the sink! And then you think it's over. But it's beginning. They follow you. They follow and follow."

"Always with that smile," said another. "And then she had the stroke. She couldn't move. And still she had the smile. I'd cry out to see it. And her eyes would fill with tears for me. For me, I tell you, for me."

"Two hours," said another. "Five months old she was. One minute she was smiling. Like an angel in my arms. And then she began to cough and shiver. It came in her eyes. She reached for me. It's like she was falling. She died in my arms. And not even a word could she say. Not one word passed between us. What's the meaning of it? But what's the meaning of such a thing?"

Grace went numb with listening and waiting. It was not until the procession gathered at the cemetery that she gave way. She was holding Fabrizze. Suddenly she was standing over it.

"O my God," she said. "O my God! Don't let it happen! Don't put him in there! Don't do it! O, Grandfather! God help him! O my God, my God! Don't let it happen!"

She collapsed beside the black open grave.

For weeks after the funeral she refused to go out of the house. Her eyes would fill with tears at the mention of his name. Night was the dreadful time. Memory was like a hand squeezing her heart. Mendone returned to invite her back into the past. She remembered the day that she had come to live with him. It was as though the wind had swept the house into disorder. And yet there was a white rose nodding in a wine glass on the kitchen table.

"I'm getting old," he said. "Have patience with me."

One night she thought of the gay lovely year following her marriage. She remembered the white gloves and the nuts and the wine. She saw him gazing at the violin in a troubled way.

"Why does this violin worry you?" said Fabrizze. "The music is in you, Mendone, and not the violin."

"But it's true, "said Mendone.

Grace sat up in bed in the dark. So sharp and terrible was the sense of loss that she gave a cry. Suddenly her body was shaking with sobs. Fabrizze put his arms around her.

He would leave in the morning and return to find her staring out the window. One day she was sitting before an open drawer that held the pipe and few belongings of Mendone. The violin and the stool were beside her.

"Is this all?" she was saying. "Is this all?"

"You should put these things away," said Fabrizze.

"My heart is like a stone," said Grace. "I think of death and death and death. This morning I woke up with an idea in my head. It made me cold. Perhaps we don't belong here."

The neighbors watched for a time and then they took a hand in it. Soon they were coming to visit her all through the day. First to arrive in the morning was Adelina. The old lady put life in the house with her stinging talk.

"Is there no coffee?" she said, in the empty kitchen. "I came with the snow, old as I am, and not even a cup of coffee to warm me. Come down here, Grace. Out of bed with you."

"I'm not in bed," said Grace, coming down.

"Why not?" said Adelina. "You might as well be."

She was rubbing her finger along the window sills and the woodwork. Paul thought it was a game. He followed her.

"You should be ashamed," said Adelina, showing the dust.

She washed her hands before unwrapping a loaf of bread.

"Someone must look after your husband," she said. "And what about the boy? Did you tell him that life was over? Tell him something else. Tell him that your grandfather lost a mother and a father. And a wife and a daughter."

"The bread is warm," said Grace.

"I'll show you how to make such bread," said Adelina.

"My aunt used to say she was building a loaf of bread. I put eggs in mine. You can make it while your neighbor sleeps."

Later in the morning Bassetti came from the market with a basket of endive. He cleaned it leaf by leaf at the sink. Meanwhile he talked and talked.

"Endive is good in a salad of oil," he said. "Better yet, you can cook it with the white beans. It's no wonder the poor people have strength. . . . It was a favorite dish with your grandfather, eh? Do you know I chose him to be one of my pallbearers? It was settled between us, and here it was I carried him. The second time such a thing happened. Do you remember the grocer's father? Spracchi?"

Bassetti waited for his answer.

"I don't remember," said Grace, softly.

"A remarkable face," said Bassetti. "How I wanted that face at my funeral. And he promised to be there. The man never smiled. He closed his mouth against it. Two deep lines worked into his face. You'd follow the lines up to his eyes. Why, it broke your heart to look at them. The man was stuffed up with grief. He used to go out of his way for a funeral. One night he was at the wrong funeral for two hours. . . . And so the endive is cleaned."

The turning point of these visits came on the morning Poggio brought his gift. It was a feather duster. Poggio went upstairs with Grace following him. He began to dust the picture of Mendone on the wall. No sound was in the room. His arm fell. He turned to Grace with a stricken look. Her eyes were bright.

"I meant no harm," he said.

"There is none," said Grace.

"My father is right," he said. "He says that everything I do is wrong. From now on I'll do nothing."

"But it's a lovely gift," said Grace, kissing him.

Sweet laughter welled inside her.

At that moment Vivolo slipped out of his room. The cane was on his wrist and he carried a black briefcase. He closed his door as if leaving the scene of the crime. He sniffed the air and was gone.

"I'm going to the store," said Poggio. "You're staying here. But where is the panther going?"

Suddenly Grace realized that Vivolo had been living in the house all through this mournful time. Never had he come to disturb her. It seemed he was being careful not to intrude on her sorrow. She felt a surge of warmth for the dark lonely man. She would invite him to supper.

Sharp at five he returned. He tapped his cane in warning and hesitated at the kitchen door. Grace put her sewing aside. When she looked again Vivolo was gone. She went out and saw him slip into his room. He closed the door without a sound.

Grace wondered about him. As time went on the mystery of his manner and purpose helped to draw her away from grief. Early in the day he left the house with his briefcase. Returning in the afternoon he took a nap. After a stroll he locked himself in his room where the light was burning long into the night. The neighborhood was fascinated by its own rumors. Misinformation was carefully pieced together. Vivolo was being watched and questioned and even followed.

One morning he stepped out of the house as Cardino was coming down the street. Cardino froze in his tracks with the look of one who is concealed. Vivolo took a golden watch out of his vest. He held it there in the sun. He studied it. He let it swing on the golden chain. Cardino followed the swing. His head was swaying with it. Vivolo put the watch away. He tapped 'the briefcase and beckoned. Cardino followed him. Vivolo circled the block and went back into the house. He had forgotten his cane. Cardino was waiting when he came out. Vivolo made a motion as if to take out the watch again. Cardino was gazing at the loop of chain. Vivolo smiled and beckoned.

"We'll go around again," said Vivolo. "And then I'll swing the watch a little."

"Once is enough," said Cardino. "I have a favor to ask. I'm going in to see Grace. Tell me what to say. Something cheerful."

"There is one blessing," said Vivolo. "The blessing is life."

"Life?" said Cardino. "But Mendone is dead."

"There you have it," said Vivolo.

"But I understand you," said Cardino. "You mean there's nothing to say, eh? What a deep one you are! Still, we get to know each other. Come closer. Tell me what's in the briefcase."

"Never," said Vivolo.

"Bravo," said Cardino, startled.

Evidence weighed against Vivolo. He lived alone and had no friends. He asked no questions and tended his own affairs. The fact is, he was becoming a kind of threat. Josephine complained that he looked at her as though he needed further proof of her existence. Adelina said he never even looked at her. No one could place his dialect.

"It's from the east coast of Italy," said Gritti. "And he has that look about him. I've seen it before. There's a cup of the icy Greek blood in him."

"Sicily, Sicily," said Poggio. "Go near him and he puts his hand in his pocket. It's to be sure he left his money home."

"He smiles and smiles," said Penza. "What's the reason for it? You leave him and it's like he put water in your shoes."

"Those eyes, those eyes," said Rumbone. "Like olives."

Rumbone was gripped by the mystery. Surely he would open the newspaper and find a picture with word that this cunning criminal had been surprised in the midst of conspiracy. Rumbone abandoned all customers when Vivolo tapped his way into the store.

"Some Brioschi," said Vivolo, one afternoon.

"Brioschi, Brioschi," said Rumbone, craftily.

"It's a clue," said Vivolo.

"I had this dream about you," said Rumbone. "I woke in a cold sweat. They were coming for you."

"The neighbors?" said Vivolo.

"But what are you up to?" said Rumbone. "Trust me, trust me. Tell me everything. Put it on me."

"Your face, your face," said Vivolo. "It tells me everything but your name."

Vivolo returned to the house. Grace was in the kitchen. He removed his derby and waited in the doorway.

"Please come in," said Grace. "Have some coffee."

"Do you have camomile?" said Vivolo. "My throat is raw."

Grace prepared camomile tea.

"You were sewing the other day," said Vivolo. "It was the first time in several weeks. I hope it means you feel better."

"I do," said Grace. "Everyone is kind."

Vivolo sipped the tea. His head was cocked. It seemed he was listening to his heartbeat.

"I've been watching Fabrizze," he said. "He keeps the others behind the counter. He works with his hands. He moves the crates and sacks. He stocks the shelves and sweeps the floor. He scrubs the walls. And all the while he watches the door."

Vivolo leaned forward. His face had the dark elegant glow of woodcarving.

"And then he gives up," he said. "He won't lift a bean. He sends for the boy who plays the harmonica. He'll sit on the sacks and listen to music the rest of the day. Last week the boy made a song for him. Just for him. Fabrizze was excited with it. He was moving all the crates again. . . . Do you know I broke a promise?"

"What promise?"

"I promised to send you to him," said Vivolo. "It's for you and Paul he's watching."

Grace woke Paul from his nap. She dressed him and went down to stay with Fabrizze until he closed the store.

NOW and again Vivolo came for an hour of talk in the long wintry afternoons. Grace was careful not to question him and so she learned nothing beyond the fact that he had traveled widely. One day he was eager to share good news. For the moment he would only reveal that he was caught up in a venture promising a success as brilliant as his talents.

"I had two ideas," he said. "But it upsets the stomach. Now I have the one. It's like an affair."

"Of the heart?" said Grace.

"Never," said Vivolo. "The heart never sleeps. Listen then. I'll be down here later. I'd like to talk to Fabrizze."

Fabrizze did most of the talking. He came home bursting with news of his own. Grace sat there trying to keep up with it. He went round and round the table.

"Here's Vivolo," he said. "Come in, come in. Sit down. A glass of wine. Did you hear the news? Things are happening, my friend. I sent a hundred dollars to my uncle in Italy. I'll send more. It will build up. He'll put it aside for the people planning to come here. They'll pay it back when they can. And I'll send it again to help others. One thing more. My uncle has two fine sons. He says he'll send them when they're older. They should come as soon as possible. We'll be ready for them."

"Wait a day," said Grace. "We need food in the house."

"There's food enough in the store," said Fabrizze. "One thing more. I'm buying fifty acres of land in the outskirts of the city. Land is cheap. I'll buy more. Some day we'll build houses there."

"Five minutes more and we'll have a city," said Vivolo.

"I was thinking of Adelina," said Fabrizze. "On the last night of the funeral I went to the kitchen. The old lady was crying. At the same time she was digging the marrow out of a soup bone. 'Poor Mendone,' she said. 'What's to be done?' And then she was at the bone. 'Why should I lose the best of it?' she said. She cleaned the bone white and then she was wringing her hands for Mendone again. 'What's to be done?' she said. She went upstairs to take a nap and be strong for the burial in the morning. She cried out louder than anyone. 'What's to be done?' she said. A few weeks later she was here every day to help Grace. An old lady and she does everything she can. It's a lesson for us."

"But what's to be done?" said Vivolo.

"I'm not sure," said Fabrizze. "Look at this. Do you know what it is? Take a guess."

"A cup of earth," said Vivolo. "A sample of the land?"

"It's from a mountain near my village," said Fabrizze.

"A cup from a mountain," said Vivolo.

"A mountain from a cup," said Fabrizze. "Let me explain it to you. I was telling Grace about it. Yesterday I woke with a feeling I used to have. A cup was full inside me. I began to rush around. I emptied the cup. A little here, a little there. A pinch here, a pinch there. I looked back and saw nothing. It was like I lost it. Today I feel better. I did something. I made plans."

126

"Stop a moment," said Vivolo. "I want you to know something about me. Can you spend a day with me?"

"It isn't necessary," said Fabrizze.

"Do you know anything about the stock market?" said Vivolo.

"Nothing at all," said Fabrizze.

"Come with me on Monday," said Vivolo. "You'll be interested. And I'd like to have you with me."

Monday was memorable.

First of all Fabrizze and Vivolo took breakfast together. They downed raw eggs mixed into cream. They drank black coffee and then they marched forth as though to slay the dragon. The street came alive at the sight of them.

"Look who's there!"

"Bravo, Fabrizze! He caught the panther!"

"Take him away!"

"Have a care!"

"Let him go first!"

"But where is he taking you, my boy?"

He was taking Fabrizze downtown to the stock exchange.

The exchange was located in a great room on the second floor of a black building. The room was already busy with people. Most of the men were down to their shirt sleeves. Women sat in high straight chairs. The focus of interest was a blackboard running from floor to ceiling on the front wall. The blackboard was covered with numbers and symbols. Three young men were going up and down ladders to change the numbers. They changed the numbers again and again. It seemed that nothing satisfied them. Another man sat on a stool in the corner. He was reading a yellow ribbon that came from a ticker with a globe of glass. It was his word that set the others dancing back and forth and up and down the ladders. Each report from him brought a change in the numbers and a comment from the crowd.

"Opening is firm."

"Tide may turn."

"Futures, futures."

"Something to set the pace."

"Steel is the key."

"Watch the utilities."

Vivolo drew Fabrizze aside.

"Do you hear the ticker in the corner?" he said. "It gives the sale and price of stock shares. The announcer calls it and these men change the prices on the blackboard. It's done in a matter of seconds. Look up there."

"At the man on the ladder?" said Fabrizze.

"Do you see him erasing that number?" said Vivolo. "Just above there you see N-S-X. It stands for Great Northern Shore Railroad."

"But I worked there," said Fabrizze.

"I know, I know," said Vivolo, smiling. "A hundred shares of it changed hands. While we talk here. It's up two dollars a share on the day. He changed the price on the board. Why were the shares sold? Someone thinks they are going down. Why were they bought? Someone thinks they are going up. You said that things were happening. But this is the place, my friend. Fortunes are

128

made and lost every day. And sometimes in an hour. The only thing sure is change. Come this way."

Vivolo found a chair for him.

"Don't leave this chair," said Vivolo. "Someone will take it and you'll be forced to stand. Sit here. Watch and listen. I'll be back for you."

Vivolo slipped into the crowd.

All day Fabrizze sat in the second row of high straight chairs. He could make nothing of the announcements. He watched the blackboard. Startling changes took place. Change melted into change. The ticker seldom stopped. It sounded more and more urgent. Hour by hour the tension mounted in the room. Telephones kept ringing. Men called advice to each other. There were sudden cries of anger and delight. Fists were raised. Above them hung a cloud of smoke in the blaze of white light.

"It's time to buy."

"On the margin."

"Bull is waking up."

"Block of a thousand."

"Long position."

"At the market."

"Shorts running for cover."

An old man was sitting beside Fabrizze. He wore a battered brown hat. The lines of his face were drawn by the swoop of nose. His pale hidden eyes followed every change on the blackboard. A friend came to whisper in his ear. The old man gave him an order.

"Sell it, Casey, sell it," he said.

"It's wise, Rafferty, it's wise."

"They're marking time," said Rafferty.

Casey went away. Presently he was back.

"Ten thousand," he said. "After that dip."

"Load up on it," said Rafferty.

"All of it?"

"Loosen up the shorts," said Rafferty.

Without turning Rafferty spoke to Fabrizze.

"How are things?" he said.

"Good, good," said Fabrizze. "Thank you."

"How does the market look to you?" said Rafferty.

"It's exciting."

"A bit ragged," said Rafferty. "Are you buying?"

"I'm just watching."

"Looking before you leap?" said Rafferty. "Good for you."

It was even more exciting in the afternoon. By then the room was packed with people. There was no longer that moment of silence for the flash of news from the ticker. Delight in the crowd carried over to drown out the words of the announcer. He was raising his voice to be heard.

"Block of a thousand," he said. "Thirty."

"A new high."

"Talk of a merger."

"Earnings improved."

"Declared an extra."

"The trend is up."

"Ticker running behind."

There was an argument about a chair in the first row.

"It's mine."

"It was empty."

"I went back to the broker."

"It's the way I lost my own chair."

Vivolo danced out of the crowd. He made a sign that everything was going well. He went back to talk with one of the men in a glass office. He came to Fabrizze.

"I put in an order to sell some stock," he said. "Do you see that man in the office? He's called a broker. He buys and sells for us. I'm selling to take a profit."

A man hurried past the chair.

"Textiles, textiles," he was saying.

Vivolo followed him into the crowd.

The announcer pointed out that the trading would be finished in half an hour. His white shirt was dark with sweat. Ribbon came into his hands again.

"Voted that split," he said.

"Sing it out."

"Three for one," said the announcer.

"Look out for that baby."

"Good for ten."

"A real performer."

"Hold on," said the announcer. "A block of ten thousand here. Up eight on the big mines. Ninety, ninety."

"Eight on the mines."

"Breaking through."

"Word was out."

"Thousand on the mines," said the announcer. "Up three."

A single roar went up from the corner. Several men

had come together. They were closing in on the announcer. They were laughing and shouting.

"Box of cigars for that."

"Do it again."

"I dare you."

"Thousand on the mines," said the announcer. "Up five."

"Listen to this."

"They struck something."

"A strike, a strike."

"Ninety-eight closing," said the announcer.

"Give us a hundred."

"Do it again."

"What is it?" said Fabrizze. "What's happening?"

Rafferty turned to give him an old sweet knowing smile.

"It must be gold," he said. "It must be gold."

VIII

VIVOLO was in bubbling spirits. He promised to explain everything at the end of the week. Meanwhile he was enjoying himself. One morning he left his briefcase in the store where Rumbone would be sure to find it. Rumbone pounced with an air of breathless excitement. Inside was a bottle containing a map. The map showed the location of treasure forty paces east of the public square and forty paces up in a black building.

Poggio slipped down .to investigate. He spent three hours there and then they chased him out. No one could follow his story.

"I'm going back," said Poggio. "They'll never keep me

away. They can throw me through the door, glass and all! It's the ticker, it's the ticker. I sat in a chair right under it. I was like a king. And then I heard it. It was in my ear and my head. It was going through me. I was sweating with it. My feet were tapping. I forgot everything. Someone left a cigar and I was smoking. The spittoon by the chair was all gold. And then it started. Everyone cried out. I shook my fist. I jumped up and down with the crowd. A man caught my arm. He said I was in his chair. I blew smoke in his face. 'Iron and coal,' I told him. He threw me out. I went home to lie down a little. And now I hear that Fabrizze is buying a ticker for the store here. Ask him. He'll tell you about it."

Fabrizze was waiting to ask Vivolo about it. Vivolo came for supper on Friday. Fabrizze poured wine and right away he began to fire questions. He went round and round the table.

"What happened on Monday?" he said. "I couldn't understand it. Not even what they were saying. And what were they doing?"

"It was perfect," said Vivolo. "And you helped me just by being there. I knew you would. What a week it's been! The market broke through again."

"Do you like your fish fried in oil?" said Grace.

"I prefer it broiled," said Vivolo. "Listen, Fabrizze. Do you know how much money I made on Monday? Take a guess. Never mind, never mind. I made over a thousand dollars."

"A thousand dollars?" said Fabrizze. "How is it possible?"

134

"It's only the beginning," said Vivolo. "Let me tell you what happened. Week after week the market was going near the top. It kept falling back. And then on Monday it broke through. It set a new high. And then another. And then another. The market is learning to fly, my friend. And so am I. I may fly away."

"Before supper?" said Grace.

Vivolo laughed in a soundless way. His dark eyes closed and the laughter turned in and flowed through his body. It seemed he was saving it for another time.

"But how is this money made?" said Fabrizze.

"A company issues stock," said Vivolo. "Wait then. Say that you wanted to open another store."

"But I do," said Fabrizze.

"I thought so," said Vivolo. "Say that you needed money to do it. You might issue shares of stock. I might buy them and be a partner in the store. Later I might sell them. Shares of stock on the exchange are bought by men called investors, or speculators, or traders. They hold the stock if they think it will go up. Otherwise they sell it."

"Sell it to whom?" said Fabrizze.

"To those who think it will go up," said Vivolo.

"And it's going up?" said Fabrizze.

"Straight up," said Vivolo.

"But why are they selling it?" said Fabrizze.

"Some will take a small profit," said Vivolo. "They have no faith in the future. They don't know how rich this country is. I tell you, Fabrizze, a giant is stirring. One of the traders used to say, 'It's beyond the realm of the im-

agination!' And then he was saying, 'It's beyond the realm!'
Now he says, 'Beyond!' It's a revelation."

"It sounds like a fever," said Grace.

"It's a sensation," said Vivolo, gravely. He drained his
glass of wine and leaned forward.

"Say it then," said Fabrizze. "Tell us what you think."

"I think the fish is done," said Vivolo.

Rumors flashed through the neighborhood. It was as
though a great whip had been cracked. Time and again
Fabrizze was asked for a description of the stock exchange. His account was as baffling as it was vivid. The
clues led back to the first clue of a black building that
ticked in the heart of the city. No one could grasp the
idea of the stocks. One thing sure, Vivolo was winning
huge sums of money. Josephine heard the word thousand
falling here and there like a cannon ball.

"Is it work?" she said. "How do they call him?"

"He calls himself a player," said Rumbone. "A player,
my dear, a player. He's playing here."

"It's the rest of you who are playing," said Josephine.

"He won a thousand dollars in seven hours," said Rumbone. "Or was it seven thousand in an hour?"

"Go away," said Josephine. "Let me think about it."

She sat rocking on the porch. She rocked and rocked
until she was dizzy with it. She gave a cry and put her
hands to her temples.

Vivolo was waving to her from the sidewalk.

"Wait, wait," said Josephine, swooping down.

Smiling, Vivolo leaned on his cane. Josephine held the

fence for support. She caught her clean little apron and covered her mouth with it.

"Come closer then," she said. "Why are you smiling? How did it go today?"

"Up, up," said Vivolo.

"You won again? Don't say you won? You won?"

"Three hundred," said Vivolo.

Josephine wiped her face with the apron.

"Or more," said Vivolo.

He reached into his pocket as though for the money. He took out his golden watch. It held the sun and blinded her. She shook it off and gazed into his eyes. Suddenly she was dazzled by the light of his golden tooth.

"Come closer," she said. "Let me look in the briefcase. Never mind! You'll finish me with it! How my heart is pounding! Wait, wait. Just one look. Do it then!"

"But I don't carry the money," said Vivolo.

"Listen, listen. I have money saved from the boarders and the wine. You won three hundred?"

"Or more," said Vivolo.

"Talk to Fabrizze," said Josephine. "Tell me what he makes of it. I leave it to him. But why is he waiting?"

Fabrizze was somewhat bewildered. Day after day he hurried home from the store to follow Vivolo with questions. Something was eluding him.

"But how much money is needed to own the stock?" he said.

"It depends on the market price," said Vivolo. "Some of it runs over five hundred dollars a share. There's one I'm studying. It costs twenty dollars a share. Two thousand dollars will buy one hundred shares. Are you listening? I'll make a hundred dollars if the stock goes up a point. I believe this stock will go up ten to twelve points in the next two months."

"But why are they selling it?" said Fabrizze.

"They think it will go down."

"And they are wrong," said Grace.

"So it seems," said Vivolo. "Listen a moment. Think of Paul. Watch him. He's full of energy. Talking and laughing. Running and jumping. Digging and climbing and pounding. He's busy all day, eh? It's the same with this America."

"Why not buy more of the stock?" said Fabrizze. "Why not buy a thousand shares? Why not ten thousand?"

"Why not?" said Vivolo.

"You say its value will increase by half?"

"Or more," said Vivolo.

"And if we bought a hundred shares we'd make a thousand dollars in two months?"

"Or more," said Grace.

"Exactly," said Vivolo. "Tonight I'll go over it again. It must be perfect."

Fabrizze lay awake for hours. Igino was playing the harmonica in the night. The last song he played was for Fabrizze. It was a song of welcome and highest hope. Fabrizze sat up.

A door opened. Vivolo slipped out of his room and down the creaking stairs. Secret thrilling laughter escaped him. There was laughter in every corner of the house.

138

"Wait, Vivolo, wait," said Fabrizze, going down. "Will you buy the stock for me? How does it look?"

"Perfect, perfect. They may even raise the dividend."

"My mind is made up," said Fabrizze. "Stop at the store in the morning. I'll have the money for you."

"We'll make a fine team," said Vivolo.

They shook hands on it.

Several days later Vivolo brought the certificate of stock to the store. Mancini framed it and nailed it on the wall. Friends came behind the counter for a close look. The color and flourish of it gave them a feeling of excitement. The certificate let it be known that Fabrizze was an owner of one hundred shares of oil stock.

"The truth is, he has ninety shares," said Poggio.

"And the rest of it?" said Gritti.

"I own two shares," said Poggio. "Fabrizze is taking the money out of my pay. It's the same with Rumbone and Mancini. They bought eight shares between them. Fabrizze shares everything."

"And what about me?" said Gritti.

"You'll be left looking out the window," said Poggio. "How can we lose with Fabrizze? Everything he touches comes alive. Think of the railroad. And the wine. And the store. Look at Bassetti."

"It's true, it's true," said Gritti.

"Wait a little," said Poggio. "Vivolo is coming with the news. I'm going out to watch for him."

Vivolo came in the afternoon with a report from the stock exchange. He strolled through the market. He

stopped to look over the fruits and vegetables. Suddenly
he held his thumb up.

"Look, look!" said Poggio. "It jumped up!"

Fabrizze hurried outside with Rumbone and Mancini.
They were cheering Vivolo. Several customers joined in
the applause.

"How far did it go?"

"Two points."

"Wonderful!"

"But what's he done?"

"A look in the briefcase."

"I don't carry the money," said Vivolo.

They marched him into the back room. Bassetti had
prepared a snack of ham and cheese and wine. Customers
drifted in.

"What's happening?"

"Where's Fabrizze?"

"Give him a glass."

"How much did I make?" said Rumbone.

"Eight dollars," said Vivolo.

"And eight tomorrow," said Rumbone. "And eight and
eight."

Fabrizze hushed them when Ravello came into the
store. Ravello had his hands in his pockets.

"Way, Fabrizze, way," he said. "Where are you? Come
out, come out. Today I brought a dollar. A bit of Romano
and nothing more. One miserable dollar, do you hear?
But where are they?"

They pounced on him and put a glass of wine in his
hands.

140

"Who didn't know it?" said Ravello. "Who didn't know it? No one shows his face for a dollar."

Poggio had Gritti in the corner.

"What ticker?" Gritti was saying. "What is this ticker?"

"Some day I'll take you down there," said Poggio. "It will be the end for you. It's like a song. You'll forget where you live. We'll never hear from you again."

The next day Vivolo turned thumbs down.

"It jumped down," said Poggio. "A day wasted."

"A setback," said Vivolo. "But it's a good sign. Rumors are going around. They started buying. They started buying in big blocks just before the ticker closed."

"Big blocks?"

"Look out when they buy the cats and dogs," said Vivolo.

"Cats and dogs?"

"Something must have happened," said Vivolo. "We'll know tomorrow. It must be good news. Why else would they be buying? It may surprise us all."

And so it did.

Vivolo came through the market with both his thumbs held high. Shouts were heard as he made his way down the aisle. All at once he was a familiar figure there.

"Here's the one in the derby."

"It went up again."

"But what is it that goes up and down?"

Their cries emptied the store.

"It jumped up!" said Rumbone. "It jumped up twice!"

"I sold the stock, I sold the stock," said Vivolo. "Are you

listening, Fabrizze? You made over a thousand dollars."

"A thousand dollars?" said Fabrizze.

"The broker's commission is paid. A thousand dollars in five weeks. It's a magic touch you have! The company struck oil! I never gave it a thought. They say it's an ocean of oil. The stock went up eight points this morning!"

They were struck dumb. They watched Vivolo. They feasted their eyes on him. They waited as though for his blessing. One word would have brought them to their knees.

"And there's more to tell," said Vivolo, winking. "You'll hear it after supper."

Fabrizze heard a great deal during supper. He heard it from Grace. She was still trying to understand it when Vivolo came down from his room. Vivolo sipped wine and listened.

"Vivolo is right," said Grace. "It is a revelation. You make a thousand dollars and never once leave the store."

"I made nine hundred dollars," said Fabrizze. "The rest of it is between Poggio and Rumbone and Mancini."

"Where is the money?" said Grace.

"Downtown," said Fabrizze.

"But how did you make it?" said Grace.

"By putting in two thousand of my own," said Fabrizze. "It's a risk. Wasn't it a risk when I opened the store?"

"But you work in the store," said Grace. "Wait then. I can't get hold of this. You made a thousand dollars. Where does it come from? Did someone lose a thousand? What good will come of it?"

"Give me a chance to spend it," said Fabrizze. "Isn't it good to have a thousand dollars to spend?"

"But you had a thousand," said Grace.

"Isn't it twice as good to have two?" said Vivolo.

"And what of the man who loses a thousand?" said Grace.

"He was playing to win," said Vivolo. "Besides, you make it too exact. It isn't a game of cards."

"What will become of this money?" said Grace.

"It all depends," said Vivolo. "It may furnish the basis for another thousand."

"And two more?" said Grace.

"A hundred more," said Vivolo. "Up we go."

"Why should my shoes be under the bed?" said Fabrizze. "It's time to be up and running a little. I have ideas."

"I know the ideas," said Grace. "You'll gather with the left hand and give with the right."

"I'll buy more land," said Fabrizze. "I'll send more money to Augustine. I'll have money to help these people when they come."

"Buy a ship," said Grace, bursting into laughter. "Buy a ship of your own. Bring them all here."

"Look who's calling," said Fabrizze. "Look who's here."

"A lovely idea," said Vivolo. "You can call for the poor in every port of the world."

"And I spoke with Mancini," said Fabrizze. "He's bringing a builder of houses to see me. Spronzi is his name. Spronzi says it's cheaper to build in quantity. Five houses will be almost as cheap as three. Ten houses all at once will be cheaper than seven one by one."

"And a thousand will cost nothing at all," said Grace. "What else did Spronzi say?"

"He heard a rumor from Poggio," said Fabrizze. "He heard that I was opening five more stores in the city. He asked for one in his neighborhood. Poggio took his address."

"Give him our address," said Grace. "Did Mancini tell you the foundation goes on sinking? Did he tell you the whole house seems to be resting on the one beam? The beam that makes a funny noise when you tap it?"

"Remember Mendone," said Fabrizze. "A bit of faith."

"Up, up, up," Vivolo was saying. "Up we go."

"Let me finish the dishes," said Grace. "And then we'll fly away together."

Vivolo took Fabrizze out for a walk. They went round the block and stopped in front of the house. Grace watched them. Vivolo was talking. He became so excited that he was dancing round Fabrizze. They set off again and returned to the same spot. They were dancing round each other.

"I didn't make a thousand," said Vivolo. "I had the very same stock, Fabrizze, but I bought a thousand shares. I bought it on the margin. I took your advice. I made ten thousand dollars!"

"Ten thousand dollars? The margin? Hold still."

"The margin," said Vivolo. "Listen then. The margin makes it possible to buy a dollar's worth of stock for ten cents. The broker stands behind you if you have a little money in reserve. You play for ten times as much simply by increasing the risk. If the stock falls, of course, you

144

have to cover the loss to keep control. But I knew it wouldn't fall. And guess what? I have another stock in mind. I've been watching it for weeks. A peach ripe on the tree."

"Hold still," said Fabrizze. "Tell me about it."

"It cost thirty dollars a share," said Vivolo. "Nine thousand dollars will buy three thousand shares on the margin. And still I'll have money in reserve to cover a break. You follow me? This stock will move twelve to twenty points in the next month. At the least! It means there's a chance to make thirty thousand dollars in a month! Thirty thousand!"

"Or sixty," said Fabrizze. "Hold still."

"Can we do it?" said Vivolo. "Can we do it?"

"We'll go together," said Fabrizze. "Let's buy it. Josephine is bringing a few dollars here. Gritti left fifty in a sock. We'll make money for them, too."

"Come to the exchange," said Vivolo. "Be there with me. We'll each buy a block of fifteen hundred shares!"

"Come inside, come inside," said Fabrizze. "We'll spend the profits with Grace again!"

Excitement gripped the neighborhood. The news was like a bonfire throwing light and warmth into every house. Rumbone and Mancini flashed the word that Fabrizze had won nine hundred dollars in five weeks. He had increased their money by half! And never once did they leave the store! And it was just beginning! And Fabrizze was still learning about it! And everyone was welcome to join in! And Poggio went even further with it.

"I gave Fabrizze nothing," said Poggio. "Not a cent. I

145

owed him the forty dollars. And now he owes me twenty. It's a miracle. We never left the store. It starts again next week. All we do is send Vivolo downtown."

A sudden breath-taking rush was on.

Friends brought money to the house on Jackson Street. Grace and Fabrizze were bewildered by the amounts. Grace tried to discourage them. They would have none of it. Their passion mounted with each warning. Fabrizze realized that he had lost control of it. Everyone had been waiting for a chance to put in with him.

Josephine started it by coming with four hundred dollars knotted into a handkerchief. Grace had to cut the knots. She was astounded when she saw the money spill forth.

"Why so much?" said Grace. "Why do you keep it at home?"

"I have more in the bank," said Josephine. "I'm afraid to go there by myself. This is from the wine and the boarders."

"Why do you need more?" said Grace. "Tell me why."

"I don't understand," said Josephine.

"Why do you need more money?" said Grace.

"But I want it!" said Josephine. "I want it!"

"Be satisfied with what you have," said Grace.

"I might as well die and be done with it!"

Poggio arrived with a handkerchief. Grace had to cut the knots. Within was another handkerchief and within was his weekly pay of twenty dollars. Rumbone came with two hundred dollars. Mancini delivered a hundred. Salupo

146

offered fifty. Penza counted out forty and then he added seventy-five cents in change.

"We'll be together in it," said Penza.

"Take back the change," said Fabrizze. "What's happening?"

"I'm going upstairs," said Grace. "It's too much for me." She missed Gritti who came with a hundred.

"I was holding it back," said Gritti. "And then I heard what Josephine was bringing. I came right over."

"Keep it, keep it," said Fabrizze. "You gave the fifty."

"I gave it too late," said Gritti. "Now I'm giving before you start again. I had the money under my father's picture. He died with a shovel in his hands. He was digging in a field. 'It's deep enough,' he said. And he fell in. I was thinking of it. And there I was with a shovel in my hands. I'm sick of it! Take the money. Do your best!"

Last to come was Cardino. He was investigating the reports. He could make no sense of what Poggio had been telling him. Poggio cornered him again.

"Here he is," said Poggio. "I figured it out for him. I have it on paper. Right here."

"What, what?" said Cardino. "What's happening?"

"It's that money you saved," said Poggio. "You worked thirty years for two hundred dollars. I figured it out for you. You're fifty years old. Listen then. You'll have a thousand dollars when you're two hundred years old!"

"Don't make him nervous," said Fabrizze.

"But what are these stocks?" said Cardino.

"Steel and oil!" said Poggio.

"Please, Poggio, please!" said Fabrizze.

147

"Tell me, Fabrizze, tell me!" said Cardino, pounding the table.

"Pork and wool!" said Poggio.

"Is it true what I hear?" said Cardino.

"It's the ticker!" said Poggio. "They'll never keep us away!"

"Madonna mia!" said Josephine. "Madonna mia!"

In the following week Fabrizze spent no time in the store. He and Vivolo bought three thousand shares of the stock. Day after day they were caught up in the smoke and fury of the exchange.

Their stock held steady. It went up a point and down a point. They had just about given up hope for the week when the stock jumped into action. It taught them a lesson. It shot up five points on a single sale. They turned away to congratulate each other. A cry went up from the announcer. The stock soared five points more.

Vivolo put in an order to sell at the market.

"I'm taking the profit," he said. "Are you selling?"

"But you said twelve to twenty points," said Fabrizze. "Wait, Vivolo, wait. Next week it will go higher!"

Fabrizze left the exchange.

He met Poggio who was being sent as a runner for news. They went to the store. Fabrizze loaded Mancini and Bassetti with cheese and ham and sausage and cookies. He emptied two cans of origan into a barrel of black olives. He tossed in a bag of dried hot peppers and put the cover on the barrel.

"Where is this going?" said Rumbone.

"To the house," said Fabrizze. "Close the store. A

breath of air. Let's be in the sun. And we'll have a party."

"Did we win?" said Rumbone. "But how much?"

"I didn't count," said Fabrizze. "Over four thousand."

Rumbone sat down on a sack of beans. He looked as if he had been clubbed. His eyes filled with tears.

Poggio hurried off to serve the last customer. The man cried out for provolone.

"How much a pound?" he said.

"Forty cents," said Poggio.

"Thirty I'll give!"

"Thirty-eight!" said Poggio.

"Thirty-two!"

"Twenty-five!" said Fabrizze. "Sold, sold!"

They were packing him off.

"What's wrong with the cheese?" he was saying.

"Nothing, nothing. Come again. Show your face again."

"You'll get me next time, eh?" he was saying.

They closed the store and rolled the barrel across the bridge. Everyone saw them coming. Poggio pointed to the barrel and flung his arms wide as though it was all over. Grace was at the window. Her mouth fell open. Paul was running to meet his father.

"Another thousand?" said Grace.

"And more," said Fabrizze. "We'll have a party."

The house creaked and groaned with it.

Fabrizze stayed in the kitchen with Bassetti. The old man was giving him a massage.

"Soon I'll have just the right touch," said Bassetti. "I'll steal the pain, and you'll never know it."

Fabrizze slipped five dollars into his pocket.

"Put it in the stocks," said Bassetti, smiling. "You bring a new language, my boy. Thousand and five thousand. Ten and twenty thousand. It's a new language for us."

From the basement came the throb of the guitar in a tarantella. The dancers shook the house. There were cries of delight. Poggio was dancing on the barrel.

Cardino carried his chair into the corner and sat in front of Vivolo. He was so thrilled by the report of the ten thousand dollars that he could think of nothing to say. He put his hand on Vivolo and leaned forward. He tried to speak.

"Why are you squeezing my leg?" said Vivolo.

"I'm sorry, I'm sorry," said Cardino.

He began to talk. Words gushed forth. He told the story of his life. He shook his fist. He was too small to make trouble and too big to hide. He kept shoveling and drinking and shoveling.

"You have no children?" said Vivolo.

"Not one," said Cardino. "Wait, wait. Come closer. Can you tell me something? Is there a way?"

"But there are ways and ways," said Vivolo.

"Tell me."

"Listen then," said Vivolo. "It will take three days and two nights. She mustn't work during that time. Every six hours a hot bath. And then she rests. She saves herself. A bit of music."

"Music, music," said Cardino. "This is good."

"A glass or two of red wine," said Vivolo.

"Red wine!"

"It's the end of the third day," said Vivolo. "She'll take

a glass of hot wine. A spoonful of sugar for the blood. She'll take another glass. And then another. And then another."

"Four glasses?"

"Or more," said Vivolo.

"And then? But don't I know? Bravo, Cardino!"

"Why are you squeezing my leg?" said Vivolo.

"Tell the rest, tell the rest!"

"Send for me," said Vivolo. "Send for me!"

Tony Cucuzza was playing another tarantella.

IX

FABRIZZE was right.

The stock went on climbing and he made twice as much money as Vivolo. He sold it. Vivolo found another stock. Fabrizze plunged in again. He was going down to the exchange with the air of one blazing a trail. Vivolo remarked that he was making an adventure of it.

"It's not good to risk everything," said Vivolo. "You should always keep money in reserve. Safety first."

"Safety first?" said Fabrizze. "But you surprise me. Safety first? We would never leave our beds."

"Listen then," said Vivolo. "You remember the oil stock? The company didn't strike oil. It was a rumor. The stock

152

went up ten points on the strength of it. And then the truth came through. Do you know what happened? The stock slipped back two points. Only two points! And then it jumped five more!"

"Why did it jump again?" said Fabrizze.

"News from the company," said Vivolo. "The company sent word it was drilling with high hope. Do you understand? It's enough that the company was drilling!"

"And nothing happened?"

"They struck oil," said Vivolo. "But you miss the point."

"They struck it," said Fabrizze, laughing. "The oil was there all the time. Good for them! And what about this new stock? What are they doing?"

"Chopping and sawing," said Vivolo, gravely. "It's a pulp and paper stock. They own so much timber land that only the sun sees it in a day. They're chopping."

"And hope is high," said Fabrizze.

"So it is," said Vivolo.

It was even higher in the neighborhood.

Sweet summer swept the sky blue for its reign of gold. The air was clear and sparkling as wine. It seemed to crackle with good hot news. Nothing came as a surprise. Tales were carried into every corner of the city. Rumbone passed along thousands of dollars with each bag of groceries sold in the store.

"Did you say thirty thousand?" said Ravello, ironically. "Why stop at thirty? Why not say a hundred? Say a million, my friend, and be done with it. Why are you looking like that?"

"I made a mistake," said Rumbone. "Why didn't I borrow money from Josephine? I'm a fool."

"You're looking at a fool," said Ravello. "Here comes a fool through the door. Fabrizze is making fools of us all!"

Thousands of dollars more Rumbone scattered in the course of his evening round of visits. One night he was bound for the house of Cardino with news and wine flaming inside him. He met Cardino coming to visit him.

"Thousand, thousand," said Rumbone. "Let's go to your house. I'll blow you up like a balloon."

On the way they met Poggio. Poggio was carrying the newspaper and panic to the house of Josephine.

"Thousand, thousand," said Poggio.

"Cats and dogs," said Rumbone.

"Up, up," said Poggio.

"Higher and higher," said Rumbone.

"The bull is running wild," said Poggio. "I'll be with you in an hour. Keep the wine cool."

Rumbone and Cardino arrived and drank several toasts.

"One more month," said Rumbone. "One more month like the last and it's all over. You'll be left scratching your head."

"But I'm giving the money," said Cardino.

"How much?" said Rumbone.

"I have a hundred dollars in the cupboard," said Cardino.

"I don't even turn my head for a hundred," said Rumbone. "A hundred? But you said it was two hundred."

"It is two hundred," said Cardino.

"How tricky you are," said Rumbone. "Is it really two?"

154

"Or more, as they say. I'm bringing it to Fabrizze. I have it ready. Come with me."

"Let me finish the wine," said Rumbone. "Down with the wine. Up with the stocks. Down with the wine."

"Look at these hands," said Cardino. "All you see is work and work and work. Last night I was thinking about it. And then I had this dream. These hands were growing. They were getting dark and strong. Dark and strong. They were doing things all by themselves. Terrible things. And then they were reaching for me!"

"You need a physic."

"Let's go to Fabrizze," said Cardino.

"Wait for Poggio."

"He'll be there," said Cardino. "He's everywhere."

It was true. Poggio was on the run with the big torch of rumor. He left everything in flames. He made the rounds before and after work as though it was a kind of mission. His first stop was for breakfast at the house of Josephine.

"Thirty, thirty," he said, bursting in.

His eyes were like diamonds behind the bloom of his nose. He kissed Josephine and loosened the knot of her apron. He let water run in the sink. Josephine turned to shut the faucet. Poggio lifted a napkin and saw freshly baked bread and sugar doughnuts. He rapped the door from the inside.

"Come in, come in," said Josephine.

"Thirty, thirty, thirty," said Poggio, rubbing his hands. "How much is twelve and twelve and six?"

"Thirty," said Josephine, pouring coffee.

"Thirty thousand then," said Poggio.

The old lady almost poured coffee into his lap. She asked him to write it down on a shopping bag. The black number was dancing. Josephine felt the old clutching pain in her side.

"Where is this pain?" said Poggio. "In the right side? Near the pocket? But you haven't heard the latest. This is the news of two days ago."

"And yesterday?" said Josephine.

"Just so, just so," said Poggio.

"But what happened yesterday?"

"How she goes to the heart of it," said Poggio. "But who knows what happened yesterday? Perhaps he seized control."

"Seized control?"

"Of it all!" cried Poggio. "Do it, Fabrizze, do it!"

Josephine made it back to the stove. Poggio pounded the door.

"And here's Fabrizze!" he cried, whipping open the door.

Josephine hurried there.

Poggio opened the ice box. He saw green onions and a ripe red tomato sitting on a cake of ice. He coughed as he closed the door.

"Let's eat and wait for him," said Poggio. "Pretty soon he'll be going downtown. We'll cheer him on. Vivolo will be wearing the new hat. Wait till you see it. . . . This coffee, Josephine, this coffee. It's like wine! An omelet would be nice with it."

"I hear your father threw you out," said Josephine.

156

"A little argument," said Poggio. "I forgot the bills again. I gave the pay to Fabrizze. They shut off the gas and lights."

"Your poor father," said Josephine. "And he can hardly move with the rheumatism."

"The other night he was waiting for me beside the candle. What a face! Eyes all blood! The veins in his neck like ropes! I was so frightened I blew out the candle and ran away! But now it's all right. I borrowed from Fabrizze and paid the bills."

"Make the omelet then," said Josephine. "Just the thought of Fabrizze makes me hungry. Can you find the eggs?"

Poggio found everything.

"A bit of green onion fried in oil," he said. "Two slices of tomato. Salt and hot pepper. A sprinkling of cheese. In with the eggs. Look at this bread! All gold and light as a feather!"

"Two eggs for me," said Josephine. "How hungry I am! Listen, listen: what's that?"

"Igino's playing," said Poggio. "It's the signal. Come to the window. Look, look: there they are! Look at the stride of them!"

Fabrizze and Vivolo were swinging by. They walked beside each other and yet it seemed that Fabrizze would spring free and be gone in the hot brilliant blue of morning. The sun poured gold on his flashing hair. Vivolo was moving in the soft sure way of a dancer. His pale gray hat was like a huge pearl.

Windows and doors were flung open on both sides of

the street. Greetings showered down. Salupo leaned out
the window in his underwear. He shook his fist.

"Way, Fabrizze! Do it then!"

"They go again, eh?" said another.

"O, Fabrizze!" said Josephine. "O, Fabrizze!"

"A clear head!"

"Take hold!"

"Good fortune to you!" said Lucia.

"Madonna mia," said Josephine, leaning on Poggio. "The
look of him makes me dizzy. He's on fire!"

"Take it all!" said Poggio.

They swept round the corner out of sight.

Poggio went to the store for a while. He left in the
afternoon and stopped for a snack with Lucia. Lucia was
pregnant.

"How are you feeling?" said Poggio. "I brought you a
bag of wild onions. You had a taste for them, eh?"

"I'll save some for you," said Lucia.

"Everything will be ready for the baby," said Poggio.
"What a time to be born. He'd be laughing if he knew. . . .
Pass the cheese."

"I felt him move," said Lucia. "He kicked!"

"It's for joy," said Poggio. "Do you know that your
husband has over five hundred dollars? I swear it! How
he's changed. He won't lift a hammer in the store. He
turns away if a customer is coughing. I have to wait on
the sick ones. He rubs his hands with olive oil and washes
them every hour. And he's ordering a new suit from
Salupo. All silk underneath. . . . I'll try the cake."

Poggio bought a newspaper and went to see Gritti. He

was reading aloud as he came through the door. The latest report was frantic and precise.

"Listen, listen," said Poggio. "The stocks went up! All the records broken! Common and preferred! Up, up, up! Steel and oil! Pork and sugar! Cats and dogs! Beans and macaroni! The bears have a bull by the tail! The bull is dragging them away!"

Gritti sat there in underwear soaked with sweat. His face was black with a growth of beard. His chin sank into the dark mass of his chest hair. Poggio danced round the kitchen. He drank glass after glass of wine. Gritti was watching him like a spider.

"How lucky you are," said Poggio. "But look at you. What have they done to you? It's like someone threw a shovelful of dirt in your face. And how hot it is in here. Wine should be kept in a cool place. It's like a furnace. But what have they done to you? Quit that job. A curse on the railroad! Fabrizze will open a store for you. But you'll open your own, eh?"

Gritti gave a cry and caught Poggio by the leg. Snarling and squeezing, he brought the young man to his knees.

"I want the truth out of you!" said Gritti. "Tell me everything! What's happening down there? The truth!"

"Stop, stop," said Poggio. "Listen then. You gave a hundred and fifty dollars. It was enough to buy seventy shares on the margin. Or more. The stock sold for twenty and jumped twenty. Or more. You made a thousand dollars! Or less. I swear it! Fabrizze has it marked down!"

"A thousand dollars," said Gritti, stricken. "A thousand."

"Fabrizze knows what you have," said Poggio. "Better

159

yet, he knows what you need. You need a cooler house in the summer. How do you stand this place? Take a deep breath. Sweat and babies and garlic. And you need a different job. Look at you. And you need a bath, I swear it!"

Poggio was already through the door.

He finished his whirlwind tour by visiting Grace. He accepted an invitation to supper. Grace was waiting for Fabrizze. No longer did she know what to expect.

"Did you hear the latest?" said Poggio. "Fabrizze is buying a big harmonica for Igino. It weighs fifty pounds. Igino will clamp it to his shoulders."

"So it's you with the rumors," said Grace, laughing.

"I lie a little and then I find out it's true," said Poggio.

"It's happening too fast," said Grace.

"I can't keep up with Fabrizze," said Poggio. "He's a wonder, Grace. Everyone speaks of him. Everyone waits for him. You should see it when he gets on the trolley. I was with him one morning. The people know him already. They nod and smile. Everyone begins to talk. The men tell him their troubles. He sent one of them to Rossi for a job. The women show him their babies. One girl was showing him her leg. She said it was sprained. Vivolo and I looked over and she called us scoundrels."

"Wait, wait," said Grace. "I hear the trolley. He's coming, Poggio, he's coming."

"Watch the corner," said Poggio, going to the window. "Watch the corner at Harrison Street. Look, look. A window goes up. Salupo is there. Josephine stops rocking. And here he comes! Vivolo is behind him!"

"It's good news," said Grace. "I see it in their walk."

"But he's coming back!" said Gritti, as though expecting that Fabrizze had been swallowed up somewhere.

Friends were gathering. They followed Fabrizze into the house. Glasses of wine were raised again and again. They watched Fabrizze. He ran his hands through his hair. The lights of gold deepened the blue of his eyes. He smiled and smiled. He aimed his finger here and there at the empty glasses. Poggio went round and round filling them from a gallon.

"He won, he won," said Cardino.

"All of us won," said Fabrizze. "Hundreds, hundreds."

"You'll go back?" said Gritti. "I can't believe it."

"They'll never keep us away," said Poggio. "Never, never."

"And tomorrow?" said Josephine. "Will it be the same?"

"It should be better," said Vivolo.

"But it's like a story," said Cardino. "It's like a story in this America."

"Take me with you," said Poggio. "Take me downtown."

"Take me," said Grace, filled with sudden delight.

"Tomorrow may be the best day of all," said Fabrizze.

So it was.

On the first day the stock went up five and down three and up four. The next morning it opened three points higher and then it jumped three more. Vivolo sold it. He put in a rush order to buy two other stocks.

"But why did you sell?" said Fabrizze. "You told me it was good and now you get rid of it."

"It's a hot potato," said Vivolo. "I don't like what's happening to it."

"It keeps going higher," said Fabrizze.

"For no reason," said Vivolo. "There was talk of a three for one split of the shares. Up went the stock. A director of the company said there would be no split at this time. Down went the stock. He spoke of a stock dividend. Up went the stock. No stock dividend was declared. The talk goes on and on. It's a conversation, Fabrizze, and the stock jumps up and down with it. They're beginning to play with these stocks. We'll have to be careful."

"And now you bought two others?" said Fabrizze.

"Why should we fool with cats and dogs? These are the blue-chip stocks. When the market moves, my friend, they climb twice as fast and far. They're holding steady. They're marking time."

"Railroad stocks?" said Fabrizze.

"The giants," said Vivolo. "They have mineral rights to the land. They have oil wells. Their earnings improve all the time. But they've been lagging behind the market. Look out. A surprising thing will happen."

It happened on a Friday.

Poggio was the first to sound the alarm. He took breakfast with Josephine and was sipping his coffee at the window. Suddenly he heard the song of the harmonica. Fabrizze and Vivolo came in sight. Abruptly the music stopped. Fabrizze was pushing a wheelbarrow down the sidewalk.

"Come here, Josephine, come here," said Poggio.

The old lady came with a handful of oyster crackers.

She was dropping them one by one, like secret wishes, into a cup of coffee. She saw Fabrizze. She heard Adelina rocking on the porch. She gaped at the wheelbarrow. Adelina was thundering. Poggio flung open the window. "Do it, Fabrizze, do it," he said. "Take it all then! Make two trips! Make three! Benedico!"

"O, Fabrizze," said Josephine, spilling crackers on the floor.

By noon everyone found out that Fabrizze had merely taken the wheelbarrow down to the store. They were beginning to relax and then Poggio was in their midst. He invited them to a party in the house on Jackson Street. It was like a trumpet blast.

Poggio had just returned from the stock exchange. The stocks were climbing. The bear was dead. The bull would never die.

"Go to the store," said Fabrizze. "Tell Rumbone to get ready for a feast. Find Cucuzza. It will be a lovely day!"

Poggio carried the word through the neighborhood. Grace heard it before he arrived.

"He's coming, he's coming," said Poggio. "All records broken! Sugar and spice! Cement and diamonds! Oil and vinegar! Tripe and sausage! Up, up, up! Come to the window!"

"Stop, stop," said Grace. "I can't sit still with you."

"Listen, listen," said Poggio. "It's the trolley! There they are! All of them! Arm in arm! Look, look! They closed the store! Look at the food! Down the middle of the street! Every day with these parades! They made a million! I swear it!"

Poggio was not so far wide of the mark.

All day the stocks were swinging higher. In the last hour of trading one of the blue-chip stocks ran up twelve points on a single sale. Ten minutes later the other stock shot up fifteen points.

The traders were swaying and chanting.

"The rails are breaking through!"

"Show the way!"

"Make up for lost time!"

"Highball, highball!"

Fabrizze was stunned. The jump in price carried him up to two hundred thousand dollars. He turned and fell into the arms of Vivolo. They made their way to the store and then home.

Long before dark the celebration was under way.

Fabrizze sat upstairs in the kitchen.

"Send for Bassetti," he was saying. "I can't eat anything. A drop of wine, Grace, a drop of wine. Send for Bassetti."

Down in the basement there was uproar.

"We bought and sold!" said Rumbone.

"Just in time!" said Poggio.

"We bought!" said Rumbone. "It's going up!"

"Higher and higher!" said Poggio.

"Up, up, up!" said Rumbone.

"Sell it!" said Poggio.

"I lit a candle," said Josephine. "A novena!"

"We'll have a high mass!" said Poggio.

"Spronzi was at the store," said Mancini. "He said there are more houses every time he comes. Make a city, he says, and be done with it!"

"A city, a city!" said Poggio. "Houses and stores! Schools and churches! Peaches and cream! Steel and gas!"

"A little white square," said Rumbone. "Piazza Fabrizze."

Salupo was measuring Cardino for a suit.

"Every stitch by hand," said Salupo. "The coat will be shaped like a bell. Silk under the lapels. Pockets of silk!"

"Make them deep!" said Cardino. "I'll want them deep!"

"I'll carry them to your knees!" said Salupo.

Dancers whirled.

Vivolo came down and was greeted with shouts.

For the moment Grace and Fabrizze were left in the kitchen with Bassetti. Grace drew up a chair.

"Can you hear me?" she said. "Do you recognize me?"

"It's my wife," said Fabrizze, pinching her.

"Do you know where you are?" said Grace.

"I'm at home," said Fabrizze. "What's happening?"

"Tell me what's happening," said Grace. "I don't understand any of this. It's like everything is coming loose."

"Things are better every day," said Fabrizze.

"Better and worse," said Grace. "There's talk of thousands and I see less money than ever. I owe a bill to the butcher. Do you know what he said? He said I shouldn't bother you. But where are these thousands? It's like a dream. Penza was here. He was talking and talking. He was spending money right and left. He's ready to send for a wife. 'Where's the money?' I said. He put a finger on his lips. I was breaking the spell."

"I'll bring the money," said Fabrizze.

"Bring it then."

165

"It's all there," said Fabrizze. "More than ever. It's piling up. I could have brought it home tonight."

"But why didn't you?" said Grace. "What does it mean? Listen a moment. Fifteen people are waiting to come here from Italy. Do you remember talking to Salupo? He had a letter from his family. The crops failed in the village. 'Tell them to be ready,' you said. He wrote and told them. Are you bringing them all here?"

"Let them come, let them come," said Fabrizze.

"Will you change clothes before they come?" said Grace. "Look at you. And when did you last eat? One thing more. Did you hear what your son is going to be when he grows up? Poggio put it in his head. 'What will you be?' they ask him, in the street. 'A millionaire,' he says. 'Or more,' he says."

Down in the basement the music started again. The guitar was being plucked in a piercing and powerful way.

"Wait, Grace, wait," said Fabrizze.

"Everyone is waiting," said Grace.

"It's happening fast," said Fabrizze. "Let me explain. Last month I made a plan to spend the money. All at once I had twice as much to spend. I made another plan. And then I had twice as much again. The money pours into my hands. I'm carried along with it. It makes me think of that last night on the ship. I woke up with a cry. I didn't know where I was. My uncle reached over and put his hand on me. 'Soon it will be morning,' he said. 'We'll be there.' He was right."

"How does it feel?" said Bassetti, massaging him.

Fabrizze was searching through his pockets to find

166

money for Bassetti. A sudden baffled look was on his face. Grace burst into laughter and gave him a dollar. He passed it on.

"Put it in with the rest," said Bassetti.

"There it is," said Grace. "It's beyond me."

The music of the guitar swept through the house like a sheet of flame. Fabrizze was tapping his feet. Bassetti shuffled in a dance round the chair.

"How this Cucuzza is playing," he said.

"Let's dance a little!" said Fabrizze.

Down they went.

"It's Vivolo playing," said Grace.

Vivolo was standing with one foot on a chair. His eyes were shut tight. His curly hair bounced on his brow. It seemed he was listening for and playing only the wildest music in the guitar. The dancers clapped and stamped the floor. They cried out. They rushed from wall to wall.

Suddenly the crowd came apart.

Gritti was on his knees in the corner. He had caught Poggio by the leg and was squeezing him down.

"Tell the truth for once!" cried Gritti.

"Your working days are over!" said Poggio.

"I'm warning you!"

"A little white square!" said Poggio.

"It's your last chance!"

"Piazza Fabrizze!" said Poggio.

X

FABRIZZE promised Grace that it would be over and done with by the holidays. He guessed right. Afterwards, no one could say just what happened in those final weeks.

Fabrizze sold the railroad stocks at a terrific profit. He was eager to buy again. It was at this point that Vivolo turned wary. He called Fabrizze out of the crowd.

"Come away from them," sad Vivolo. "Close the door. It's a choir in there and you'll be singing the same song. Let's wait a little and watch the market. What's the hurry? Do you know how much money you have? Two hundred thousand dollars!"

"But why wait?" said Fabrizze. "We'll miss out!"

"I have a feeling," said Vivolo. "A feeling of danger. Summer is over, my friend."

"Look at the market," said Fabrizze. "It's going up. They say it's the fall rally."

"How quick you learn," said Vivolo. "But I know about the fall rally. It's the rally that comes between the summer rally and the winter rally. They rally from rallies. I tell you it worries me."

"Why do you worry so much?" said Fabrizze. "You worried about the oil stock. It climbed ten points after we sold it. You worried about the paper stock. It's nineteen points higher. And the railroads are still going up."

"Wait then," said Vivolo. "There was a stock here selling for ninety dollars a share. You know what happened on Friday? It shot up thirty points. An increase in value by one third. In one day! And it's a good stock. I have hope, Fabrizze. But this is where faith comes in. I don't believe it."

"But it happened!"

"It shouldn't happen! It means that the stock was thirty points off its value. Why should the stock be thirty points off when everything else is so high? Consider the railroad stocks. I studied them. I looked for a fairly wide move in six or eight weeks. They went up thirty points in an hour!"

"And they're up again!"

"A kite will go up even if you keep it on a string. Cut the string and it goes higher. But it belongs to no one."

Fabrizze refused to listen. He insisted on making one last investment. Vivolo picked the best stock on the list.

"Buy it outright," said Vivolo. "Buy it on a long-pull basis. Never mind the margin. The stock costs two hundred dollars a share. Buy a thousand shares. Pay cash and forget it."

"Is there a good chance the stock will go up?"

"They call it a bellwether," said Vivolo. "It will lead the market up or down. I just don't know about it. Nothing looks the same to me."

"It's because you have so much to lose," said Fabrizze.

"I'll tell you a secret," said Vivolo. "We can sell short and make just as much money if the market falls."

"And if it goes up?"

"We lose, we lose."

"Do you mean it?" said Fabrizze. "We'd be sitting and waiting for bad news. Like two funeral directors. I'll buy again. I want more than a thousand shares."

"Buy four thousand then," said Vivolo. "It's a twenty-five per cent margin. I'll talk to the broker for you. I'll make him think I'm standing in with you."

"Do it then," said Fabrizze. "Come in with me."

"Get in with the choir," said Vivolo.

The purchase of a block of four thousand shares carried the stock up fifteen points. It meant a quick stunning profit of sixty thousand dollars. For a time the market soared with it. And then it stopped. It seemed to be frozen right there. It went up a fraction and down a fraction. The exchange came alive with rumors.

"It's marking time!"

"Solid as a rock!"

"Coast is clear!"

"Strike for new highs!"

"Talk of war!"

"Wars, wars!"

"How strong and steady," said Fabrizze. "Look out, Vivolo, look out. We'll fly away."

"I sold short a little," said Vivolo.

It was a time of breath-taking hope. Day after day Fabrizze sat in the white smoking light of the exchange. He paid no attention to minor advances in the stock. One afternoon he was halfway home before realizing that a fractional gain of three quarters yielded a profit of three thousand dollars. He was thinking of a million. The word was big and sweet as a plum in his mouth.

Late in the night he would send for Adelina and Bassetti. The old man came to massage him with warm olive oil.

"Sit easy, sit easy," said Bassetti. "Lean forward then. You sit back and back like a lion."

Adelina sat beside him at the table. She thought a spell was on him. Poggio thought she was laying it. She let three drops of oil fall into a saucer of water. Presently she was whispering and making the sign of the cross on his brow.

"It's no wonder you don't sleep," she said. "You're on fire."

"It's a fever," said Grace.

"Poggio says he's like a torch," said Bassetti.

"The torch is going out," said Grace.

"Be careful," said Fabrizze, pinching the women. "You'll catch what I have!"

"We caught it," said Grace.

"Sit still then," said Bassetti.

"Josephine is just as bad," said Adelina. "And this Rumbone! He's losing his mind!"

"You'll need a bicycle to make the rounds," said Grace.

Rumbone knew that Fabrizze was in the midst of a final daring assault. For the moment it was a deadlock. Everything was hanging in the balance. One afternoon he rushed Vivolo into the back room of the store.

"Why are you here?" said Rumbone.

"Where should I be?" said Vivolo.

"It's early," said Rumbone. "Why are you sweating like that? Something happened down there! I knew it!"

"Calm yourself," said Vivolo.

"But where's Fabrizze?" said Rumbone. "Where's Poggio? Is it true what I hear?"

"You mean Piazza Fabrizze?" said Vivolo.

"Please, Vivolo, please! I can't think straight! I get so excited I have to lie down! I can't rest! I get up again! And up and down and up!"

"Like the stock," said Vivolo. "Listen a moment. Monday was a good day for Fabrizze. And for you. But nothing has happened since then. Keep your fingers crossed. You'll know very soon. It may be a matter of days."

"A matter of days!"

"Or less," said Vivolo. "Or less."

One look at Fabrizze told the tale.

"He's with us like a tiger," said Poggio.

Suddenly he would be there in the lovely soaring light of morning. Igino filled the day with song. The street rang with shouts and laughter. Fabrizze saluted each of his friends. He made big circles in the air with his right hand. It seemed he was dancing down that leafy aisle of gold. Now the song was over and he would be gone in the perfect autumn blue.

Everyone had turned away by the time Vivolo slipped out of the house. No longer would he share in the applause.

Fabrizze returned in the haze of afternoon. The little eager bell of the trolley told of his coming. He was still on the march. Vivolo lingered at the corner. Igino played as though the song was bringing Fabrizze. Friends and children poured into the street. Vivolo stayed in the shadow of the red rooming house. Fabrizze was dancing beneath leaves weaving their gold on the sky.

The neighborhood was swept up in that last blaze of excitement and wonder. Hope ran so high it would be remembered as a time of fulfillment. It was known that Fabrizze had risked everything. A million was at stake. And more. Poggio spread word it would be over by the end of the week.

So it stood as Fabrizze marched away on that Thursday.

"We are all here!" he cried, making a circle in the air. And then he was gone.

There was music and laughter. There was talk of a feast to end all feasts. Rumbone and Mancini were celebrating before noon in the back room of the store. Adelina and Josephine rocked and rocked on their porch. They threw coins to the sidewalk so that the children might buy ice cream. Cardino left work early to see Salupo about his new suit of clothes, and a gallon of wine hidden in the big red

173

box in the closet of the attic. Cucuzza was there. They drank the gallon of wine and emptied the box of toys. They swore to carry the party right on through the weekend.

Cardino was dancing in his underwear when Poggio brought that first warning about the stocks. Poggio had just come from the exchange. He was bewildered by what he had seen.

"It's Poggio!" said Salupo. "Silk and salami!"

"The news, the news!" said Cardino. "Out with it!"

"Up with it, up with it!" said Salupo.

"How pale," said Cucuzza. "Wine for him."

"I was there," said Poggio, helplessly.

"Tell us, tell us!" said Cardino.

"It's changing," said Poggio. "It's changing."

"What's that?" said Cardino. "It's a lie!"

"It's jumping down," said Poggio. "I swear it!"

"No more of that!" said Cardino. "Don't listen, don't listen! Get hold of him! No more of that!"

The commotion brought Gritti up to the attic. Everyone was in hot pursuit of Poggio. Gritti drank a glass of wine.

"Tell the truth!" cried Cardino.

"I told you!" said Poggio. "Wake up!"

"Lies, lies!" said Cardino.

"Get hold of him!" said Salupo.

"Don't listen!" said Cardino.

"It's different, it's different!" said Poggio.

Gritti went down and started to shave in the kitchen. He kept hearing the words of Poggio. All at once Igino

174

was playing the song of welcome for Fabrizze. Igino lived in the rooms below.

"Way, Fabrizze, way!" said Gritti, at the window.

No one came swinging round the corner.

Gritti resumed his shaving. Igino was playing. Gritti looked out the window. He turned away with a curse. The music started again. He slashed his chin with the razor. He plunged downstairs.

"Stop it, stop it!" he cried, pounding the door. "Come out of there! Are you losing your mind?"

The music started. Out of instinct Gritti lunged to the window in the hall. He almost went through it.

"Look at the blood!" he cried, cupping his hand under his chin as though to save it. "Poor me, poor me! Look at the blood! It's a bad sign! A curse on Poggio! Come along, Fabrizze, come along!"

It was the first time that Fabrizze failed him.

The stock market had broken.

Fabrizze was at the exchange when it happened. Within three hours his own stock fell twenty-two points. The rest of the market crumbled with it. There was panic. Men jumped out of their chairs and scurried from corners. A woman screamed. Wild cries filled the air. Phones were ringing. Brokers left their offices. Everyone came together in a rush. The crowd was closing in on the announcer as though to bring him down. The ticker kept on and on with quick neat reports of falling prices.

"Landslide!"

"Unload, unload!"

"Sell at the market!"

"Get me out, get me out!"

"Sell, sell, sell!"

Fabrizze sat there watching.

Vivolo took his arm and led him into the hallway.

"Listen, Fabrizze, listen," said Vivolo, trembling with excitement. "Wake up, wake up! There's a chance for you!"

"But what's happening in there?"

"Never mind," said Vivolo. "Listen to me. Part of your loss was a profit. Seven or eight thousand covers it. You'll keep control of the stock. I'm giving you the money. I'm putting it in for you. It's possible the stock touched bottom. Tomorrow it may bounce up. I don't believe it. But one good move *is* all you need! Eight or nine points! You can sell and salvage what you put in!"

"I can't take the money as a gift," said Fabrizze.

"Don't be a fool!" said Vivolo. "I put it in already! I can't lose either way! I made five times as much!"

"I'll borrow," said Fabrizze. "I'll borrow the money!"

"Why should you borrow?" said Vivolo. "Take it from me and forget it. I tell you it's a waste. I'm giving you the money! It's only that you have a quarter of a million to protect! It isn't right for me to lend and put this debt on you! Try to understand!"

"I'll borrow from Rossi!" said Fabrizze.

"You don't listen!" said Vivolo. "I'm giving it to you on the spot! I've already given it!"

"I can't take it," said Fabrizze. "Not in that way."

"Go back inside," said Vivolo. "You ask what's happening? I'll tell you. Fear is happening. You haven't seen the end of it! ... But where are you going?"

"To get the money," said Fabrizze.

He went to the railroad yard and found Rossi. Fifteen minutes later they were hurrying to the bank. They arrived just before it closed. Rossi drew out his four thousand dollars. He insisted that Fabrizze come back to the house with him.

"I have a hundred more," he said. "Here it is."

"Keep it, keep it," said Fabrizze.

"Go to the store," said Rossi. "Take what's there."

"I'm borrowing against the store," said Fabrizze. "The store is yours if something happens."

"How is it mine?" said Rossi. "It's our store."

"Let me tell you about this," said Fabrizze. "I can't believe it. Let me explain to you."

"Do you have to explain?" said Rossi. "I have the money and I give it. And that's all. Take a glass of wine before you go."

Fabrizze leaned forward.

"I'll sign a note for you," he said.

"O, Fabrizze," said Rossi, softly. "Shame on you for once."

"It's only right," said Fabrizze.

"Listen to him," said Rossi. "I wish I had a million dollars to give you. Don't you know we'll do anything for you? My heart feels as big as a ham when I'm with you."

Rossi put his hand on Fabrizze.

"And I'm ashamed of myself," he said. "Do you know

why? Because I felt so happy to be able to help you. And all the while it's going bad for you."

"It is," said Fabrizze. "I'll borrow more on the house."

"But it takes weeks," said Rossi. "Think, my boy, think. Why are you going so fast with this?"

"I need the money by tomorrow," said Fabrizze.

"They were talking of a million," said Rossi. "Why do you need money if you have so much?"

"To hold what we have," said Fabrizze. "I don't understand it myself. If I could only tell you how strong I felt this morning. And then it started. The stocks were falling to pieces before my eyes. I sat there watching with all this strength inside me. There was nothing I could do to stop it. I sat there!"

Poggio came in. Fabrizze gave him a quick complete account of the break in the market. Poggio sank into a chair.

"I guessed it," he said. "You mean we lost it all?"

"Not yet," said Fabrizze. "Not yet."

"O, Fabrizze," said Poggio, stricken.

"Sit up straight," said Rossi.

"O, Rossi," said Poggio. "Did you hear him?"

"There's a chance for us," said Fabrizze.

"O, Fabrizze," said Poggio.

"Let me feel a bone in you," said Rossi.

"I need money," said Fabrizze. "I need money."

"He needs money," said Poggio. "Listen, listen."

"We can save everything," said Fabrizze.

"You need money?" said Poggio. "Wait, Fabrizze, wait. She'll save us! Go to Josephine! Josephine has money! In the bank!"

178

"We'll see her in the morning," said Fabrizze, pounding the table. "Go there now. Prepare her a little."

Fabrizze went home. All night he sat and talked with Grace. They drank three pots of coffee. Poggio came back. They had breakfast together in the dark of morning. Grace was questioning Fabrizze until dawn.

"Yesterday was a mistake?" she said.

"It caught everyone by surprise," said Fabrizze. "It must be happening somewhere else. There's no reason for it."

"No reason you can see," said Grace.

"All at once they were afraid," said Fabrizze. "It was spreading like a fire. The first bad day in months and no one was ready for it. Today should be different."

"It might be worse," said Grace.

"How could it be worse?" said Fabrizze.

"Talk to Vivolo," said Grace. "He says it will go down again for sure. Call him and ask him."

"And what if he's wrong?"

"When was he wrong?"

"He's right until he's wrong," said Fabrizze.

"But he even knew it was going to fall. He told you."

"Listen then," said Fabrizze. "I'm risking a few thousand to protect a quarter of a million dollars. One good day and we'll be out of it. All we ask is to recover the loss of one day. Part of it, part of it. Think of our friends who put money in."

"I've been thinking of them," said Grace. "All night."

"But what are you telling me then?" said Fabrizze.

"Why must you borrow?" said Grace.

"Do you want me to fold my hands here?" said Fabrizze. "It's lost unless we put money in."

"I want you to think before you act," said Grace. "Why should you throw money away? Two days ago you had more money than anyone could ask for. You never used it. And now you borrow to save it. You'll pay for something you never even used. Why should you throw more money away?"

"Because I have it," said Fabrizze.

"But you don't have it!" said Grace.

"Josephine has it," said Poggio.

"Wait then," said Grace. "Isn't it better just to borrow and give these people their money?"

"It isn't right," said Fabrizze.

"It's better than nothing," said Grace.

"What about the rest of the money?" said Fabrizze. "Are you telling me to give it up? I can't do it! I'll do everything I can to save it! I know it will be better today! I know it!"

"The strength is in you," said Grace. "And not there."

"I'm going to Josephine," said Fabrizze. "Come along, Poggio."

Grace called him back from the porch.

"Give me a kiss then," she said.

"There's one thing," said Fabrizze. "It would be a knife in my heart to wait and tell these people it was finished. I wouldn't know what to tell them."

"I'll be waiting for you," said Grace.

Josephine was bustling in the kitchen. Her eyes were

bright with love and delight. Fabrizze sat down and gestured to indicate Poggio would do the talking.

"Here we are," Poggio was saying. "Do you remember I told you last night? Didn't I tell you?"

"You did tell me," said Josephine. "Good morning, Fabrizze."

"I told you I'd be here early," said Poggio. "Here I am. And I told you Fabrizze would come. Here he is. Always the truth. We came for the money. Quick, quick. Money for Fabrizze. Fabrizze for money. Money and Fabrizze. Fabrizze and money. It's Fabrizze for money, and money for Fabrizze!"

"Stop it," said Josephine. "Sit still."

"We'll return it next week," said Poggio. "More than you lend. Next week for sure. Sit up straight, Fabrizze. How tired he is. But he never sleeps. Money, money."

"Why doesn't he talk?" said Josephine. "How white he is!"

"He's nodding, he's nodding," said Poggio. "Let me look in his pocket here. A handful of money! Money, money!"

"Put it back!" said Josephine, goggling.

"And the other pocket," said Poggio. "Benedico! Still another handful! What a mastermind!"

"He needs more?" said Josephine. "Why does he need more?"

"For the back pocket," said Poggio.

"Stop, Poggio, stop," said Josephine. "It's a serious thing. I heard this rumor. Tell me what happened yesterday. Is it true the stocks jumped down?"

"They go up or down," said Poggio. "Do you want them

to go sideways? And why are you talking about yesterday? Today is the day. Today, today! Look at Fabrizze.
Look how excited. I promised not to tell it all. He can't
even talk about it!"

"Speak, Fabrizze, speak!" said Josephine. "Will you
bring the money next week? And the other, too? Can you
bring it on Tuesday?"

"Tuesday, Tuesday," said Poggio. "Tuesday is perfect!"

"Be sure it's the afternoon," said Josephine. "Now and
then I go out for a walk. I may not be here in the morning."

"We may not be here in the afternoon," said Poggio.
"What is it?"

"Money, money," said Poggio. "It's all settled for Tuesday. Fabrizze is nodding! What a bargain she drives!"

"Will you speak a little, Fabrizze?"

"It may not be on Tuesday," said Fabrizze. "But I'll
surely pay it back. All of it!"

"Enough then," said Josephine. "We'll go to the bank.
I have five thousand dollars."

She bathed and wore her finest black dress for the occasion. She clapped on her black hat like the half shell of
a great walnut. Poggio polished her black shoes.

"And now what?" he said. "A flower in your hair?"

The rest of it was a blur.

It took an hour to get in and out of the bank. Josephine
was caught in the revolving door. She refused to let go
of the bar. Round and round she whirled. She was dizzy
with it.

"Come out, come out," Poggio was saying. "There's no time to lose! Let go then!"

Josephine was whimpering. Poggio had to go in after her. He helped her into the bank. The interior struck her dumb. Marble columns soared into the pale misty light. The floor was like a frozen sea. There was an air of hushed expectancy. Josephone was trembling. She took hold of the bars of a teller's cage. She was afraid to move. The vast door of the vault was closing. It sent shivers through the floor. A whirring sound was heard. Bulbs of light were flashing. The door sealed an entire wall. Josephine was holding her breath. She gaped at the teller. He was sorting money. Money, money, money. He was up to his elbows in it. His nostrils dilated. Such disdain in his face! Josephine passed water.

The policeman staggered and cried out. There was uproar. A crowd gathered. Fabrizze and Poggio were in the middle of it. An official rushed to the scene. He worked his way through the crowd. He saw it all in a flash. He worked his way out of the crowd. He looked as if he had been sucking a lemon.

"Never, never," he was saying. "Never in my experience! A run on the bank and now this! Take her away!"

"Let go," said Poggio. "Come this way."

Josephine gave a heartbreaking sob.

"Gesu, Giuseppe, Maria!" she cried.

"Never, never, never!"

"Get a doctor!"

"A mop, a mop!"

"Take her away!"

Josephine let go when they gave her the money. She wanted to leave a hundred dollars in the account. They insisted that she take it all. Poggio eased her through the crowd. She gave a cry when he released her into the door. All at once she was caught there again. People were streaming in and out.

"Let go," said Poggio, from the sidewalk. "Now, now!"

Round and round she went. Her eyes were glassy. She let go at the wrong moment and popped into the bank. She was there holding the cage again. She gaped at the teller. A crowd gathered. Poggio said that the policeman pulled his gun.

"She's back!"

"Here's the other one!"

"Take them away!"

Josephine shook her fist and cursed them.

"Animals, animals!" she cried.

By this time Fabrizze was taking the money downtown. Within two hours he was ruined.

The market opened firm. It seemed to be taking hold. There was a spurt of buying. Cries of hope were heard.

"Correction is over!"

"Cleaned up the shorts!"

"Resumes the upward swing!"

"On our way!"

It collapsed before noon.

The stock owned by Fabrizze fell twenty-seven points. Fifteen minutes later it plunged twenty-nine more. The broker threw it off at the market. All was lost for Fabrizze. The rest of the numbers on the board were melting away.

The ticker never stopped. It was singling them out for ruin. Outrage and horror greeted every drop in price. Men burst into tears. There were cries of betrayal and conniving. Two men fought each other with their fists.

So it ended.

The neighborhood waited in vain for Fabrizze.

A chill wind swept down from the lake. No longer was Igino playing. One by one the lights were going out. Now and again was heard the old forlorn creak of rocking chairs. Adelina and Josephine waited on the porch until dark. Adelina left her sister there and went inside to make a loaf of bread.

Vivolo returned to the house just before midnight. Grace was waiting in the kitchen. All day she had been telling friends that the news would be bad. One look at Vivolo confirmed it.

"Where is he?" she said.

"He'll be coming," said Vivolo.

He went to his room.

Grace sat before the window. She was listening with all her heart for the wild sure step of Fabrizze. A splash of lightning revealed Cardino white and ghostly in his underwear. He had come to his window for a last look. Summer was over. Grace turned away with tears in her eyes.

Vivolo came in and sat down. He poured wine into a glass.

"Two days and it's over," said Grace. "Two days."

"It happened fast," said Vivolo. "It's too early to say just what happened."

"I knew it," said Grace. "I knew it when he left this morning. I had this feeling."

"He stopped to see Rumbone," said Vivolo. He drained his glass of wine and filled another. "He wouldn't leave the exchange until the ticker stopped. A terrible day and he never closed his eyes to it. You should have seen him. He almost fell when he got up. His legs were asleep. He went to the window and opened it. My broker dived for his legs. 'Don't do it!' he said. 'I wanted a breath of air,' said Fabrizze. We went out for a walk."

"He lost everything then?" said Grace.

"I couldn't help him," said Vivolo. "We would have gone down together. I was going to cover the first break and then the bottom dropped out. The broker sold it to save himself. . . . I made a million in two days."

"At least it was possible to win," said Grace.

"After ten years," said Vivolo. "Ten long years. And it's a strange thing. I may be the only one in the city who guessed that the market would break. I warned Fabrizze of it."

"I know it," said Grace. "He warned me. And then he warned me not to believe it."

"We were sitting in a restaurant," said Vivolo. "He showed me the list of people who put money in. Day by day he was marking down what they won. Rumbone had over ten thousand dollars. Penza had a thousand. Josephine had over twenty. I told him to burn the list. He burned it there. It made him sick. It made him sick just to think of these people. One thing more. He says he's leaving the city for a time."

186

"Leaving the city?" said Grace. "I don't understand."

"He borrowed four hundred dollars from me. He wants you to pack a few things and be ready when he comes."

"But why?" said Grace. "There's no reason for it."

"He lost the house," said Vivolo. "Right now he's talking to Rumbone. Rumbone will sell the house to pay Josephine. And then he'll sell the land and divide the money among the others. This husband of yours is thorough. He wants to leave here at once. Tonight, Grace, tonight."

"But why must we leave?" said Grace. "We'll start again. It will be easy. And there is something I didn't tell him. I'm going to have a baby."

"I told you he was thorough," said Vivolo.

"All our friends are here."

"But they were counting on him," said Vivolo. "He thinks it best to go away for a while."

"How will it help?"

"Nothing will help," said Vivolo.

"Is it better to turn away from them?"

"It isn't that," said Vivolo. "They were counting on him. It's hard to put into words. It's like everyone was up and running a little. Do you remember when he spoke of that? It will be easier if they don't have to see him and ask questions. What is there to say? I agree with him. Wounds will heal. Soon they'll be watching and hoping for his return."

"I wish he changes his mind," said Grace.

"I was trying to change it," said Vivolo. "I knew how you'd feel. I offered to pay the debts. But he is set on leaving. Perhaps it's one of the reasons he borrowed on everything."

"I'll talk to him when he comes," said Grace.

"May I have more wine?" said Vivolo. "Do you realize that I haven't even counted my money? I made well over a million. Take a glass with me."

Grace poured the wine. Suddenly she was afraid to look at him. She could feel his dark steady eyes.

"I was thinking of something," said Vivolo. "I saw Fabrizze coming tonight if he'd won. There would be a celebration. I came like a thief. And now I leave like one."

"Are you leaving?"

"There will be nothing here for me," said Vivolo.

"But where are you going?"

"Around the world," said Vivolo. "It means nowhere. But I'll rest and see different things.... Let me drink a toast to the days I spent here. A string of jewels to carry with me."

"We'll miss you."

"Before I forget," said Vivolo. "Fabrizze will know that everything is all right if he sees you on the porch swing. He says he remembers another night."

"I'll go out then."

"Don't worry about him," said Vivolo. "Now he'll be sure of what he has. I would trade places with him. But he's done with trading, eh? Listen then. I'll be leaving here in a few minutes. I packed my bag yesterday. I'll take a room in town until my things are in order. There'll be too many questions after you go."

188

Vivolo drained his wine and stepped to the door. He was tapping his right foot. His dark eyes were bright.

"What if you have a baby girl?" he asked. "What name would you give her?"

"I don't know," sad Grace. "I don't know."

"There was a girl in my village," said Vivolo. "We used to walk together. She died when she was seventeen. Her name was Fantina. I liked it."

"I'll call the girl Fantina," said Grace.

Vivolo was gazing down as at a grave.

"Many lovely things," he said.

XI

THE neighborhood was astounded by the
sudden disappearance of Fabrizze. Indeed, the shock was
so great that no one believed it. Friends hurried to the
house on Jackson Street. The old place was warm and alive
with his presence. True enough they had heard the reports of disaster on the stock exchange. But it was over.
Surely Fabrizze would be there to tell what happened and
to show a secret startling way out of it.

"Come to the basement," said Rumbone. "Fabrizze
buried wine. He wants us to have it. And there's a barrel
to be finished."

"Drown me in it," said Cardino.

190

"Where is he?" said Josephine. "Why isn't he here?"

"He'll be coming," said Rumbone. "First he wants to pay the debts. I'm selling the house and land for him."

"You mean he lost everything?" said Gritti. "I can't take it in. I can't believe it."

"It's a serious thing with these stocks," said Rumbone. "The newspaper tells about it. Everything is falling."

"But what are these stocks?" said Cardino.

"When is he coming?" said Josephine.

"How could he lose everything in two days?" said Gritti.

"Because he risked everything," said Rumbone. "He borrowed to save your money. He borrowed on everything he owned. He lost the store, too. Ask Rossi."

"I can't believe it," said Poggio. "I have the bottle here and the cork is stuck. I can't take it out."

Rumbone sold the land in the suburb. He took the nine hundred dollars to Josephine. The old lady was suspicious. She thought it was some sort of bribe.

"I'll take it," she said. "But I believe nothing. Poggio says the stocks are jumping up again."

"It's too late," said Rumbone. "Listen then. There'll be more money for you when I sell the house and furniture. Fabrizze says we should take what we like and sell the rest. I took the dictionary to remember him."

"Tell Fabrizze about the stocks," said Josephine. "And let me know when he comes. Send for me even if it's in the night."

It took a month to sell the furniture. Rumbone stalked each customer. He asked searching questions. He wanted to be sure that the tables and chairs were going into the right hands.

"Five dollars for a kitchen chair?" said a man. "Are you out of your mind? Who sat there?"

"Why do you shout?" said Rumbone. "I'll tell you the news, my friend. The price to you is ten."

"Ten? Ten?"

"Shout, shout," said Rumbone.

"Keep the chair!"

"I will keep it," said Rumbone.

Last to go was the furniture in the bedroom. A German came with his wife and son. He took the dresser and lamp and table. He came again and was bouncing on the bed. His eyes glittered. He looked at his wife. Her eyes glittered as she squeezed her son's hand. The boy kicked Rumbone in the shin and challenged him with fearless blue eyes.

"This is good," said his father, bouncing. "How much?"

"A thousand dollars," said Rumbone.

He gave the bed to Mancini.

The crowning blow was the sale of the house. Nothing was left for Fabrizze. Worse yet, no one could explain how the house fell into the hands of Fasano. The strategy of Rumbone was baffling.

"Who didn't know it?" said Poggio. "Rumbone fought for three days over the spoons and forks. He almost came to blows over the cups and saucers. And then he gives the house to a man like Fasano. We'll see about this."

Friends gathered in the street on the dark day that Fasano took possession. Adelina was wringing her hands.

Josephine gave a sob. There were tears in the eyes of Lucia. Bassetti watched with his hands hanging helplessly at his sides. Poggio sat brooding on the porch swing. Fasano gave him an ugly look and went inside.

He found guests. Gritti and Cardino and Rumbone were drinking wine in the basement. All night they had been drinking. They were trying to finish the last barrel. Fasano cursed them. He chased them out. Rumbone staggered into the crowd with a cup held tight against his hip.

"What's in that cup?" cried Fasano. "It's mine! This is all my property! I bought everything here! Stop that man! What's in that cup? Thief, thief!"

It was the cup of mountain earth from the Abruzzi.

The next morning winter came in a black rush. The trees were blown bare. Strange clouds swam up like whales to swallow the sun. A sick feeling of loss crept through the neighborhood. Every heart swelled with longing to see Fabrizze and hear from him a word of shining hope. They spoke of him as of a child stolen away. It was a bitter thing to look at the house on Jackson Street. The shades were drawn. The gate was locked and the swing had been removed in the night.

"Swinging is for children," said Fasano. "I don't swing here and so no one swings. And I'll get my cup. No one plays tricks on Annibale Fasano!"

He was wrong. The best news of the day was that someone had thrown a rock through his window. Tied around the rock was a note telling him there would be no peace in his life until he found the stolen cup. Poggio reported the news. He reported it to Cardino an hour or so before it happened.

"One thing more," said Poggio. "Annibale stopped at the store this afternoon. I was there to serve him. He wanted cheese ground up for spaghetti. He made me so nervous I dropped a piece of soap in the grinder. A good thing it was the white soap."

"Tell me what happened to Fabrizze," said Cardino. "Where is he? Why isn't he here to tell us something?"

"He's coming," said Poggio. "First he'll pay the debts. The house and land brought forty-four hundred dollars. Or more. All of it went to Josephine."

"I have this feeling," said Cardino. "I have this feeling he left something for me. What is this feeling?"

"He left word for you," said Poggio. "I'm here to tell you the sun never sets. Can you remember? The sun is always shining!"

"It's better to talk to myself," said Cardino. "Go home. Take some Brioschi. Your system needs cleaning out."

"Wait then," said Poggio. "I was with Fabrizze the last day. He said you must gather all the money you can. Beg, borrow, steal. There'll be another experiment with the stocks in the spring!"

Cardino closed his eyes.

"What a day, what a day," he said, wearily. "I was looking in the mirror. Do you know what I saw there? An old man. Look how gray I'm getting. How gray, how gray!"

"How black it is among the gray," said Poggio.

"I went to work with Gritti," said Cardino. "I was watching him. It's like I was seeing him for the first time. What a face! All dark and lumpy like a stew."

"You're talking about Gritti," said Poggio.

"He was watching me," said Cardino. "I could feel it. 'Look how gray,' he was thinking. He took my arm. We helped each other to the tool shed. We sat in the corner and talked. We were trying to understand about Fabrizze. Rossi found us and sent us home."

Cardino drained his wine and leaned back in the chair. He was gazing at Poggio. Poggio fell right in with it. He watched Cardino. His eyes opened wide.

"How gray it is among the black," said Poggio.

"Brioschi for you," said Cardino.

A time of trouble had come. It seemed that everyone was in pain. Cardino complained of hot flashes in his legs. Now and then he had the curious feeling that he had sprung a leak and was losing his strength little by little. Gritti dreamed that he had been hit by a boxcar and for weeks he was aching all over with it. Mancini broke out in a rash. Bassetti was so exhausted that he fell asleep wherever he sat. His appetite was gone. He prepared a new list of pallbearers. Adelina was taken with dizzy spells. Josephine had two teeth left and they kept her awake at night. In the morning she had the old throbbing pain in the side near the pocket. Poggio had to lie down a little.

There was no help in the rumors going round. It was known that Fabrizze had promised to return. Now came word that he had never left. He was nearby watching them. Mysterious notes were flooding the neighborhood. Gritti received one with instructions to look on his doorstep at midnight on Sunday. He was warned to keep it secret. There would be "a surprise of green as a reward for your money and your trust and that other money, too, all of it."

"Can it be?" said Gritti. "A surprise of green? How he puts things! But it's a trick! I'm sick of everything!"

Sharp at midnight he opened his door. He flung it open with the awful cry of a man plunging into darkness. Before him was a basket of endive.

Josephine was on the list. She heard that a package would be delivered by a pair of loyal friends. The package would "fill the empty places, my dear, like a music." It was delivered by Rumbone and Poggio. The old lady was breathless as she fumbled with string and three layers of brown paper.

"The empty places," she said. "He was waiting then!"

"Cut the string," said Poggio. "Cut it, cut it."

"How exciting," said Rumbone.

"He was waiting," said Josephine. "He was waiting!"

They reached the choral stage by the time Josephine unwrapped the shoe box. She tore off the lid. Within was a length of pepperoni. A last hasty bite had been taken. Josephine turned away. She dragged herself into the closet and shut the door.

"O, Fabrizze," she wailed. "Look what they've done! Where are you then? What's to become of us? O, Fabrizze!"

"Come back, Fabrizze," said Poggio, lamenting. "The coffee is on. The stocks are jumping up."

"All that money," said Josephine. "Poor me, poor me!"

196

"Cheese and bread," said Poggio.

"O, Fabrizze," said Rumbone, from the depths. He was bringing a quart of wine from the cellar.

"Tomato and pepperoni," said Poggio.

"It's like a dream," said Josephine. "But where are you?"

"Come out and I'll tell you," said Poggio.

There was silence. Josephine came out.

"I believe nothing," she said, grimly. "I believe nothing until I hear it from Fabrizze. And that's all."

"You're making a mistake," said Poggio. "The mistake, my dear, is in thinking that Fabrizze is gone. He never left. He's living in disguise around the corner. He's disguised as Salupo. And sometimes he goes as Bassetti."

"Fabrizze went back to the Abruzzi," said Rumbone. "I know it. I feel it in my bones. I'm writing this letter to Augustine. We'll find out for sure. And besides, I want a wife. It will be a bad winter without Fabrizze. A bad winter."

Rumbone wrote the letter. He gave a stirring account of his brilliant progress in the New World. He asked for a wife.

"Let her be sound in health," he said. "A clear eye and full lips. A soft voice. She should be happy in the mornings."

Rumbone told the story of the stocks. Suddenly he charged that Augustine was hiding Fabrizze in the mountains.

"We know he is there," said Rumbone. "And he belongs with us. Never mind that our savings were wiped out. Yesterday is behind us. We will save again. Fabrizze is welcome to the money! Tell him so. Tell him to come home then. We are taking up a collection. We want him here for the holidays."

There was a long rambling letter in reply. Rumbone read it to a gathering of friends. Augustine made it clear that the success of Rumbone came as no surprise. Where was the barrier to such a blend of passion and intelligence? Things were different in Rivisondoli. Passion there was, and guile enough, but all doors were bolted fast. As for a wife, Rumbone would surely get what he deserved.

At length Augustine informed them that he was hearing about Fabrizze for the first time.

"What are these stocks?" said Augustine. "I swear to you that Fabrizze is not here. If he comes I will send him to you with my sons. Two fine boys I have. Fabrizze told me to have them ready. I packed their things. All in one bag! They have nothing but hope. Poor darlings. I had them doing little exercises to be strong for this America. Now it is the end. Winter is here. An avalanche of snow. We are struck dumb. All day we sit by the kitchen stove."

Augustine begged them to have patience with Fabrizze. All at once he cried shame. The thought of his nephew took him prisoner. He wrote in glowing terms. It was like a poem. Augustine trembled with warmth in his icy corner of the world.

"Tomorrow lies before you," he said. "And I say that you will soon have word from Fabrizze himself!"

Augustine went further. He swore that Fabrizze would return to them. How could they doubt such a thing? How happy he would be in their place! How he envied them in beautiful America! How sick it made him to sit and sit by the stove!

"I am in chains!" he said. "Send something for the holidays!"

There were excited cries.

"Did you hear him?" said Gritti.

"Read it again," said Adelina.

"I'd like to see him," said Penza.

"A collection for Augustine," said Poggio.

"But he says there'll be word from Fabrizze," said Josephine.

They drank to it.

And it was so.

A letter came to Rossi before the holidays. Fabrizze was writing from Chicago. It came as a shock. So absorbed was everyone in the speculation about him that it would have come as a shock to hear he was anywhere at all.

The letter was passed around. Few of them could read and yet it was a delight to follow the sweep and flourish of the writing. Fabrizze belonged to them once more. Everyone wanted the letter and in the end everyone had it. Poggio made copies to fill the demand. The details varied.

"I see my name!" said Cardino. "What's written here?"

"Fabrizze had this dream about you," said Poggio. "He dreamed that the seas turned to wine. And where were you? You were left right here to repair the switches. But you were smiling through the tears. How proud he was!"

"Your father is right," said Cardino. "We should take up the collection and send you away."

"Seriously then," said Poggio. "Fabrizze says that each one of us is born with an empty barrel. We have to fill this barrel with trouble and then it's time for happiness. Fabrizze sends thanks to you. Why? You helped to fill his barrel!"

It was necessary to go to Rossi for information.

"Fabrizze wants me to talk to McGuire," said Rossi. "He's looking for work on the railroad."

"But this is foolish," said Adelina.

"Tell him to come home," said Josephine, scolding.

"He'll come to us in good time," said Rossi. "Debts must be paid. All was lost. Rumbone must write and let him know how much the house and land brought. He went away to see things clearly. He's trying to understand it."

"What is there to understand?" said Josephine. "He was doing well. It's the last two days that were bad. Tell him it was good until the last days."

"Listen to the rest of it," said Rossi.

"Look after the sisters," said Fabrizze. "Let Bassetti spend his time in the store. And you should open another store. Gritti and Penza and Cardino will work hard for you. Keep Poggio where he is. If you hold him to six days a week, Rossi, he will come about three. Put him on three days. He will come two? Put him on two then. Take what he is giving.

"In the coming year Grace will have a baby. I explained to her that it would be a bad time. She understands me. She agrees with me. 'And now who will tell the child?' she says. Enough then. Soon we will be together again. How we miss you! All our love."

"He'll be here in the spring," said Poggio.

"But what happened to Vivolo?" said Rumbone.

"He says nothing" said Rossi.

"I miss this Vivolo," said Rumbone. "The man was pepper in my soup. Pepper in my soup."

Fabrizze wrote again shortly after the turn of the year. He was working as a foreman on the railroad. The letter made everyone feel that he was just around the corner.

"Keep grading," said Fabrizze. "Leave the torch on. Everybody lift. How easy it is when we help each other!"

"They put him on as a foreman," said Rossi. "On the first day the supervisor was taking him around the yard. A gang of men was trying to move a boxcar to the siding. They were pushing and singing. One of the men was singing louder than the rest. He looked like Poggio. The others pushed and pushed. They couldn't budge the car. They began to shout and curse. The foreman was screaming at them. Fabrizze went in front and found a pebble under each wheel. The car moved away. Fabrizze will do well, my friends. He sends this fifty dollars to Josephine."

Josephine was soon receiving money at regular intervals. The charm of it began to wear off. Each letter brought assurance that another letter would come. The old lady was troubled. Poggio would find her with the letter in her lap.

"He sent money?" said Poggio.

"Thirty dollars," said Josephine. "It makes me nervous, God bless him. Tell him to send no more. Let him come and work here. How I long for the sight of him! Look, look. He made a picture of Adelina and me. Rocking on the porch."

Her dark eyes filled with tears.

"Do you know what happened this morning?" she said. "A bird flew in the window. A wild bird. It's a bad sign."

"What do the birds think when we are out?" said Poggio. "It's a sign of spring and nothing more. Fabrizze will come to us in the spring or the fall. He gave his promise."

"And if I die?" said Josephine.

"It's for you to decide," said Poggio. "I advise you to wait a little. Fabrizze will surely be here."

Feeling ran high in the neighborhood. It was best expressed by Gritti in his encounter with Fasano. Fasano had a face white and tight as a fist. He was a butcher in the market and on his way home he would open his coat to sicken the neighbors with an apron covered with blood. Dogs followed him.

"Hard times are coming," Penza would say.

"Don't tell *me*," said Fasano, bitterly.

"It looks like rain," Cardino would say.

"Don't tell *me*," said Fasano. "I see things for myself."

The strange stubborn man had been hearing everywhere about Fabrizze. Late one night he was drinking wine with Gritti. They sat alone in the kitchen. Gritti went over and over the excitement of the past year. Suddenly he was glum and silent.

"Is that all?" said Fasano. "You should carry a gun."

"Why should I carry a gun?" said Gritti.

"Why?" said Fasano. "You can fire salutes to this Fabrizze when there's nothing more to say."

"Will you take something to eat?" said Gritti. He sensed

an argument and wanted to be sure his guest was given every courtesy to that point.

"Nothing to eat," said Fasano. "Let me tell you I'm sick of this Fabrizze. The man changes from day to day. Wait, cumpare, wait. What does he look like?"

"Hair like fire," said Gritti. "His eyes were blue. His nose came at you straight. It was good to be with him. One day I had this headache on the job. 'I wish I could reach out,' he said. 'I wish I could reach out and take it from you.' He took it. But it's coming back. Right now."

"He doesn't even look Italian," said Fasano.

"How does an Italian look?" said Gritti.

"Backwards," said Fasano. "I'm among them and see it clearly. Don't tell *me*."

"You're the one who asked," said Gritti, ominously.

"Most of it's made up," said Fasano. "Why isn't he here?"

"He'll be coming," said Gritti. "He's in another city. They say he'll come in the fall."

"What city, what city?" said Fasano. "First he was coming in the winter. And then the spring. And now it's the fall. In the fall it will be the winter again. I'll tell you a secret. Nature is on your side. Wake up! Don't you know they've been saying the same thing for weeks? I think it's all lies! And I tell you in your face. He'll never come back, this Fabrizze. Why should he? I'm ready to leave myself!"

Fasano burst into raw angry laughter.

"A city west of here," said Gritti.

"Are you making a fool of Fasano? I'm a simple man. Meat and bread. This Fabrizze is too rich for my blood. And another thing. I know who's playing tricks on me.

He works in the store. The one with a nose like a pepper.
I found soap in my cheese. He sent a doctor to the house
at three in the morning. I wasn't even sick. And the man
wouldn't go away. I gave him a dollar for a bag of pills.
They almost ruined me. You want to hear more? There
was a dog locked in my cellar. A mad dog! You think it's
funny?"

"I heard it was a puppy," said Gritti.

"A puppy, eh?" said Fasano. "The beast jumped at me
and tore the apron off! But I know who's behind it! What's
his name?"

"Vivolo," said Gritti.

"More lies," said Fasano. "But it's as easy as breathing
with you people! You're in it together!"

"Take something to eat," said Gritti, urgently.

"Nothing, nothing," said Fasano. "Not a crust! I'm
stuffed up listening to you!"

Suddenly Gritti was holding him in the chair. He poured
wine for Fasano and then emptied the bottle in his own
glass. He waited for the last drop.

"It's a made-up story," said Fasano. "You put more wine
in your glass, eh? Why are you holding me?"

"Drink, drink," said Gritti.

"Why are you holding me?" said Fasano. "You stop my
blood! Why are you humming? Don't tell me about Fabrizze! Take your hand away! What's this humming?"

Gritti hit him a quick neat blow on the head with the
bottle. Fasano slumped forward. Gritti propped him at
the table.

"Tell me," Fasano was muttering.

204

"Fabrizze was here," said Gritti. "He's gone. Soon he'll be with us. Now you've been told. And never call me cumpare. Never, never, never!"

Spring came to remind them of the gay flashing days of the recent year. Sweet with hope was the time and it was made perfect by the long letter from Fabrizze. He saluted each of them by name; and then he announced that he was sending to Italy for his cousins.

"Why not?" said Fabrizze. "Let them come, let them come. I am longing to see them. Augustine tells me that they have nothing but hope. What more do they need? Soon after they arrive we will return to you.

"Years ago in the village we used to hear a trumpet first thing in the morning. They were bringing figs and plums and oranges up the mountain from the lowlands. A man blew the trumpet to call us to the square. I would jump out of bed and hurry there to see the sweet fresh things. The man with the trumpet had a black moustache and cheeks like apples. 'Is everyone here?' he said, one morning. And then I knew that I had come just to see the faces of my people. Now I hear this trumpet again. And Grace is hearing it. It calls us home to you. Patience then. Igino will be the first to know when we are coming. One day he will be playing and we will be together again."

Poggio was thrilled by the letter. Now again he was on the run before and after work. One morning he found Josephine watching the corner at Harrison Street. Igino was playing. The little bell of the trolley was ringing. Tender leaves were kissing and nodding on the clear sky. Josephine was nodding with them.

"I caught you," said Poggio, coming in. "Why are you blushing? Hope is free."

"It's a shame," said Josephine. "It's a shame he doesn't come to us on such a morning."

"There'll be another."

"I'm growing old," said Josephine, mournfully. "I'll be dead and gone if he waits to pay what he owes."

"But he'll be sending twice as much," said Poggio. "It will be half the time."

"I'm sick of the money," said Josephine. "It's like a curse."

"Let me tell you a story," said Poggio.

"Before you eat?" said Josephine.

"Before I eat," said Poggio. "I'll earn my bread."

"Make me laugh then," said Josephine.

"I was talking to a man called Pipino," said Poggio. "It's two years his wife is dead. Have you heard of Pipino? He plays the big accordion. So big he has to strap it around his shoulders."

"You mean the barber on Fulton Road," said Josephine.

"The very same," said Poggio. "He sent to Italy for his wife. The match was made through the mail. Pipino was older by fifteen years. When she came he was waiting at the station. He saw her in the crowd. How ashamed he was! She had this black hair and the face of a little girl. He was an old man! He wanted to hide. He closed his eyes. And then he began to play the accordion. And the next thing he knew she was beside him. He looked at her. It was going to be all right with them."

"But she died," said Josephine, wringing her hands.

"She died giving birth to a girl," said Poggio.

"She's dead, she's dead," said Josephine.

"Pipino left off mourning and you begin," said Poggio.

"Poor child, poor child," said Josephine.

"Listen then," said Poggio. "One night he was drinking in the room. He strapped on the accordion. He began to play. The music broke his heart. He drank a quart of wine. He was breathing so hard it sent shivers through the accordion. The thing was playing by itself. He went to the window and threw it out. The strap was caught on his shoulder and he went down with it. He broke a leg."

"Stop with this story," said Josephine. "What's happening?"

"And so night after night he was left in the room with his leg in the cast. The baby would cry. Pipino sat there with his hands in his lap. One night he was drinking. The cast was squeezing him. His leg was on fire with it. He started to play the accordion to forget the pain. How he played! The baby stopped crying. All at once the pain was gone! He stopped playing. The baby was crying. His leg was in flames. He started playing. The pain was gone. He kept playing. Louder and louder! He woke all the neighbors. Something got in him. He had this feeling that the whole city was listening to him. And now what if I told you that I heard it? All the way from Fulton Road. I swear it! I sat up in bed on that very night. I heard it! And then I couldn't hear it. And I was straining my ears there."

"And you heard it," said Josephine.

"It's the truth," said Poggio. "I was telling him about it. And I was telling him about Fabrizze. You know what he said? 'You had a fine ride with this Fabrizze, eh?' he said. 'But it was a fine ride!' I said. And he said something more. He'll bring the band from the church when Fabrizze comes home. It will be like a feast day. We'll string lights up and down the street."

"I like that," said Josephine.

"One thing more," said Poggio. "This Pipino is going to play the accordion tonight. But why am I telling you? You'll hear it."

"If I hear it," said Josephine.

"How stubborn you are," said Poggio. "Open your heart. The music is there. I tell you I heard it."

"You hear what you hear," said Josephine.

"But it's there," said Poggio.

And so it was.